CROSSING WORLDS

BY ZOE SAADIA

The Highlander
Crossing Worlds
The Emperor's Second Wife
Currents of War
The Fall of the Empire
The Sword
The Triple Alliance

Obsidian Puma
Field of Fire
Heart of the Battle
Warrior Beast
Morning Star
Valley of Shadows

Two Rivers
Across the Great Sparkling Water
The Great Law of Peace
The Peacekeeper

Beyond the Great River
The Foreigner
Troubled Waters
The Warpath
Echoes of the Past

Shadow on the Sun
Royal Blood
Dark Before Dawn
Raven of the North

CROSSING WORLDS

The Rise of the Aztecs, Book 2

ZOE SAADIA

For more information about this book, the author and her work, visit
www.zoesaadia.com

ISBN: 1537350226
ISBN-13: 978-1537350226

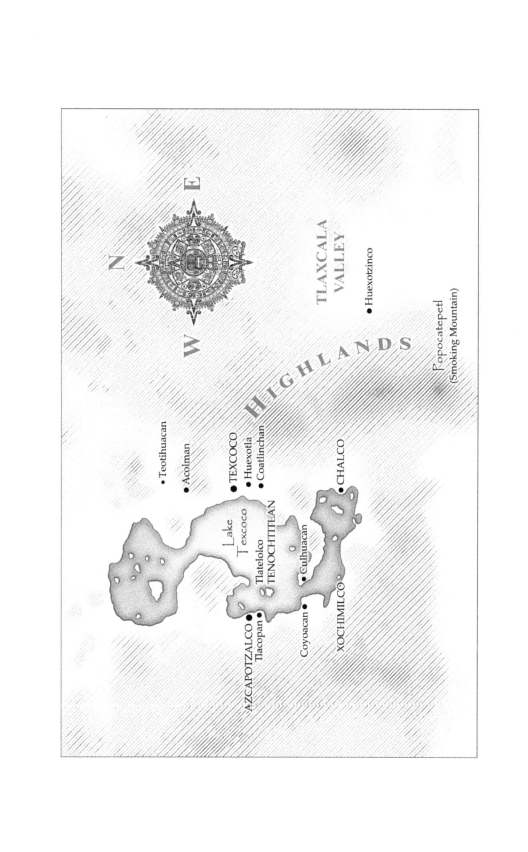

CHAPTER 1

Huexotzinco,
the Highlands,
1418

"What did you think you were doing?" Mino, the priestess of *Itzpapalotl*, the Obsidian Butterfly Goddess, glared at the girl, enraged. "What were you thinking?"

Her audience studied the floor, ignoring the clearly rhetorical question.

Trying to calm herself, Mino took a deep breath, eyeing the late autumn flowers that covered the stone altar of her goddess, wondering how to deal with the situation. Flowers offered to the mighty *Iztpapalotl*, in one of the Goddess's main temples? It was ridiculous.

"Did you do this on purpose?" she asked finally.

"No," whispered the girl.

"Then why?"

The girl straightened her gaze, suddenly calm and in control. "I just thought it would be pretty."

"What?" Exasperated, Mino flipped her hands in the air, seeing the little thing wincing, shifting backwards as if about to be struck.

"Listen," she said, trying to sound calm. "I'm not going to hurt you, so stop acting scared. But you must understand one thing. If you did this in all innocence, it's worse than if you had done it on purpose. I can't let you near our Sacred Grove temples anymore.

You will have to stop your training."

The girl took a step back, her huge eyes flooding with fear. "No, please," she whispered. "Please."

They were alone in the low stone building, and the late afternoon sunrays drew pretty patterns on the cracks of the old floor. Poor thing, thought Mino. No family, no friends, surrounded by strangers, and now, with no priestly training. But how could she keep a girl who had committed sacrilege? Unwittingly, or on purpose, it didn't matter.

She studied her painfully thin company once again. Why would someone try to cover the goddess's altar in flowers? she wondered. Was there a deity that was content to be worshipped that way?

The memory surfaced. But of course! *Matlalcueyeh*, the *Green Skirt Goddess* of rivers and streams, worshipped in the regions around the Tlaxcala Valley. Sure enough, the girl had come from somewhere around there.

"Did people of your village worship the Green Skirt Goddess?" she asked.

The girl's eye clouded. "I don't remember. Our town had many temples."

Mino pursed her lips. Countless summers of holding a prominent position, serving the powerful goddess, had taught her to read people like they were drawings on a bark-sheet. Especially artless girls. In her lifetime she had trained many, and not only youngsters, but all gamut of different pupils, and this one was obviously lying.

Her rage welled, but she tried to keep it at bay, still pitying the girl. Huexotzinco had shown kindness to all sorts of refugees, especially their neighbors from the Tlaxcala Valley. This girl had appeared here some summers ago, still a child, among a few others who had managed to escape the Lowlanders' raid on their village. Their settlement had been burned to the ground, but for some reason they had chosen to flee to Huexotzinco and not deeper into their valley, a more logical choice given their origins.

As the time passed, the refugees had become absorbed in the local life, but not the girl. Her name was Dehe, and she was a strange little thing, spending much time in the woods, keeping to herself, saying little. People shrugged and let her be, pitying the poor child. Many families had offered her shelter, but she did not get along with any of her benefactors. She was too strange, too unfriendly, too independent to arouse sympathy.

And that was precisely why Mino had taken the girl into the priestly training. She wanted to give her a chance to find her inner peace. The girl had reminded Mino of herself at about the same age, as bitter and not belonging, although much better off. When Mino's village had been sacked, she had been captured and led straight to the Texcoco slave market.

Suppressing another bout of pity, she shrugged.

"Go away, just go. I cannot let you stay near the Goddess's temple anymore. I will not punish you, although I should. What you did was despicable, and it was not done in all innocence. You are lying to me. I can see that." She took a deep breath. "I don't want to think about the other times that you may have done it and gotten away with it. Luckily, you've been caught, and I will never let you near this or any other temple, as long as I serve our Sacred Grove. I will make sure of that, although I will not notify the priests about what you have done. They would want your blood for that. Rightfully so!" Pressing her lips, she stared at the small frightened face. "After all you've been through, you don't need any more mortal punishment, although the Great Goddess will have her revenge on you in her own time. But now go, go away. Do not argue with me, because my patience is wearing off."

She listened to the frantically fleeing footsteps as they rang softly against the old stones of the floor where the grass did not sprout too thickly. What to do?

Clenching her palms to stop them from trembling, she went toward the altar, eyeing the pretty flowers spread all over the cracked rock. The rich autumn colors glowed merrily in the afternoon sun, intermingling with the brownish old stones, reeking of the old, congealed blood, enhancing its powerful grimness in an odd way.

Tlaxcalan Green Skirt Goddess, of all things, thought Mino, shaking her head. The goddess of streams and rivers. The only goddess to be worshipped with flowers and not a drop of animal or human blood. How odd.

"Honorable Priestess." The women hesitated in the doorway as if afraid to come in, eyeing the flowery mess, wide-eyed. "The Honorable Priest is on his way."

"Good." Mino turned to them briskly. "We'll have to conduct a purification ceremony, and it will have to be done tonight." She watched their faces twisting with disappointment. "Yes, I know. But we have no choice. I want to be back home as much as you do."

"Oh, yes, I could imagine that," said one of the women, smiling. "The War Leader and his warriors were rumored to come back this afternoon."

Mino frowned, but let the remark pass. This woman had served her temple for many summers and was entitled to some familiarity with the main priestess. And she had been right, of course she had. Oh, how she longed to run back home, leaving her duties behind, the moment she had heard that his warriors' party had returned. She loved her busy and demanding life, loved being the main priestess; she had worked hard to achieve this position. Yet, sometimes, she wished she could lead the life of a simple Highlander woman, because her time was never her own. Even when not busy with rites and ceremonies, people would always come to her, seeking advice or help with her herbs, needing to talk, to confide in her, the priestess of the powerful goddess, and the Chief Wife of the War Leader, mother of four prominent hunters and warriors, leading men in themselves, grandmother of many. Out of her five sons, only one had not made a name for himself.

Her stomach twisted, like always, when she thought of Kuini, her youngest. Where was he now? she wondered, watching the curtained niches around the altar, not seeing any of it. Such a wild, restless spirit, he had left more than two summers ago, angry and disappointed, mostly with his father, finding out the truth about this outstanding man in the worst possible way.

Oh, how she wished she would have known what to say to the angry youth. Had she only found the right way to talk to him on that day, two summers ago, when he had come back to life, recovering from his wounds, still weak, but so upset, so angry, so *unreasonable*.

Had she only been able to find the right words to make him see that there was nothing wrong with his father's origins. Her man might have been born a Tepanec, might have been brought up in the Great Capital of Azcapotzalco, but he had changed his way of life, and he had followed his choice ever since, excelling in what he did, working hard and doing his best to better the circumstances of her people.

Her chest tightened and she looked up resolutely. "When the Honorable Priest arrives tell him what happened, but don't tell him we know who did this. Assist him in everything he might need, and tell him I'll be back before dusk."

Resolutely, she turned around and hurried toward the entrance, not waiting for them to comment, and not wishing to see their know-it-all smiles. She could make her way home and be back before nightfall. She'd have to run all the way up to the town, but she could do it. She was not that old.

A little over fifty summers, she thought, making her way up the invisible trail. Oh, she *was* old! Yet, she didn't feel that way. In fact, she felt younger than ever and very lighthearted and light-footed now that she was about to see him after a whole moon of his absence, since he had led his people into the Lowlands.

A whole moon of longing and worry. Texcoco *altepetl* and its provinces were more dangerous than ever, abounding with warriors eager to fight, restless and agitated, tottering between their sense of triumph after humbling the mighty Tepanecs, and the acute fear of the Tepanec retaliation.

Oh, she had been worried sick, although her husband was the best Warriors' Leader in the whole world. It seemed that no force could defeat, or even hurt him, and the leader who would be able to best him was yet to be born. Still, the Lowlands were a dangerous place for the Highlanders to raid. Or to run around the way her son must have been doing for these past two summers. She took a convulsive breath. Whatever Kuini was doing he was not dead. If he was, she would have known, somehow.

The delicious aroma of roasted meat spread to great distances, and she knew her sons and some of their numerous wives must have invaded her house to organize a welcome-home feast.

She didn't mind. A priestess of her status should not be forced into running a household, even if it did belong to the powerful War Leader who did not have an adequate amount of wives. To take no additional women was his choice, although she welcomed it eagerly. Why would she wish to share him with unimportant, even if useful, hands and faces?

Short of the entrance, she stopped to regain her breath, unwilling to let people see her all flustered and gasping. Many voices flowed in the cool evening air. The women's chatter gushed more rapidly than usual, and the men sounded louder, more agitated. She neared the patio and watched them, unnoticed for a moment. So many people! She could see the women rushing about, distributing plates, serving the men, who squatted upon the mats or strolled around, entering the house or coming out of it.

He sat in the company of five of the most prominent leaders, eating heartily, tearing a piece of roasted meat with his large white teeth, all of them still in place despite his advanced age.

How handsome he looked, she reflected, watching him as he listened to one of the men. Age suited him, adding calm dignity to his narrow, foreign-looking face. His eyes twinkled lightly, reflecting amusement, but she knew he had listened attentively, remembering it all, weighing everything carefully and thoroughly. Her man was deeper than he cared to display.

"The Lowlanders will throw the Tepanecs back into the Great Lake, the way they did two summers ago," claimed one of the leaders. "They gained enough fighting experience running all over the enemy side."

Raising his eyebrows, the War Leader wiped his mouth with the back of his palm. "I'm not as certain they'll be successful this time. Two summers ago the Tepanecs came here arrogant and ill prepared." He shrugged. "I suspect they have learned their lesson."

"Oh, Honorable Priestess!" The women rushed toward her, eager to pay their respects. "We wanted to send word to the Sacred Grove, but Ino said to proceed."

"I thought we could manage without bothering you, Honorable Mother," said Ino shyly. Mino liked this plump sweet-natured woman, the first of her eldest son's wives.

"Please, come inside. We have a nice little gathering of our own in there," said another of her sons' wives, smiling.

Fighting her irritation at being interrupted while listening to important things, Mino smiled. "I have to go back to the temple, girls. I came over to greet my husband after his long journey, but I won't be able to stay for your lovely celebration."

"Do you have to go back now, when it's getting dark?" asked an elderly woman, one of the other leader's wives.

"Yes, regretfully so. There is something important that should be attended to this very evening."

They all stared at her wide-eyed, and she felt incredibly silly. Of course, it did not make much sense to come the long way from the Sacred Grove just to interrupt the great leader's conversation with a formal greeting. She should have guessed he wouldn't be alone and waiting. Determined, she went toward the squatting leaders.

Nihi, her eldest, saw her first. Smiling reservedly, the impressive man nodded and half rose from his mat.

"Greetings, Mother," he said quietly, unwilling to interrupt the conversation of his elders and betters.

One after another, they turned their heads, nodding politely, their smiles distant, wondering at the purpose of her interruption. However, all she could see were *his* eyes, beaming at her, his joy at seeing her spilling over, unreserved, not bothering to conceal it, oblivious of acceptable customs, as always.

"This is the sight I've missed seeing since coming home this afternoon," said the War Leader, springing to his feet, as light and as agile as a young man. He caught her arms. "How were you, wife?"

For a moment, she was afraid he would hug her in front of everyone, or maybe just sweep her off her feet, to carry her into the house, to make love in the way he liked. He could do anything, this husband of hers. She fought her own smile from showing. He never bothered with customs and traditions. He was a stranger, a foreigner, and his strength, one of his many strengths, was in his not attempting to conceal it. He did not know all the customs, and he wouldn't be bothered to try and live up to anyone's expectations. He couldn't care less.

"How was your journey?" she asked, relieved to see that he hadn't planned to hug her in front of everyone.

His eyes lost some of their amused sparkle. "Interesting, very interesting."

She frowned, watching him, knowing the signs. "Well, I won't interrupt you—"

"You are not interrupting. If you wish to grace us with your presence..."

She could feel their disapproval spreading like a cloud, enveloping them. "Oh no, I have to go back. I just wanted to greet you upon your return."

"Then I'll walk you out," he said resolutely.

Not bothering with anymore pleasantries or explanations, he put his arm around her shoulders, propelling her toward the muddy road outside their small garden, leaving his influential companions behind, to wonder and shrug. But, of course, they all knew him too well by now to be taken aback.

"So you made your way up here in quite a hurry," he said, once out of the people's sight. "Is everything well?"

"How do you know I was in a hurry?"

He laughed. "You have this glow about your cheeks, the glow of a person who has run uphill quite a long way." He measured her with a teasing glance. "In other words, you are all flushed and sweaty."

"Oh!" She narrowed her eyes, then grinned. "Is the Great War Leader complaining?"

His grin was wide and unabashed. "On the contrary. The Great Man is flattered and pleased to see the Honorable Priestess of the

Mighty Goddess running all over the woods just to catch sight of him."

She caressed his arm. "I wish our guests would go away."

"Shall I throw them out?"

She shook her head vigorously, half afraid he would do just that. He could do anything, this man of hers.

"I have to go back now. Back in the temple, there is a serious matter we have to resolve. But I hope to return before the last of your guests leave," she added hurriedly, sensing his disappointment.

"Can't it wait until tomorrow?"

She frowned. "Of course it can't."

"Then I'll go back to my guests," he said lightly, not offended.

"Tell me what's wrong." She looked at him searchingly. "Something is amiss, isn't it? You've been away longer than you planned, and all those people did not come here just to greet you."

His eyes lost some of their good humor. "Yes. The Tepanecs. They are coming back, and this time I predict they are coming to stay."

She felt it like a punch in her stomach. All at once, her lungs emptied of air and were not able to get it back fast enough. Fighting for breath, she looked at him, feeling her palms tightening around his rough, muscular arms, maybe even hurting them. The memories of her village, her people, her youth, oh such a long time ago, swept over her. *The Tepanecs were coming!* However, his palms were squeezing her shoulders, firm and warm, giving her strength, the way they always did.

"No need to get frightened," she heard him saying. "It won't change anything. Not for a while, and by the time it might, we'll be ready. They will never take Huexotzinco."

"But they'll take the Lowlands?" she asked, her own voice difficult to recognize, so hoarse and strangled it sounded.

"Yes, I think they will, this time."

"Why? Texcoco managed to repel them two summers ago. They threw the Tepanecs back into the Great Lake, and then they invaded their side of it. Why couldn't they do it again?"

His face darkened, became older. Grim, he looked more his

age, the man who had seen more than fifty summers, the leader who had won countless battles, father of many sons and grandfather of more.

"I know the Tepanecs," he said finally. "They may lose a battle, but they will never lose a war. They take whatever they want, even if it costs them an effort of more than a few summers to do that. They are as relentless as a lethal whirlwind, and as unstoppable. They are a menace." He pursed his lips. "I told our people we should have helped the Lowlanders for a change, but they wouldn't listen. And it's a pity." A humorless grin flickered. "After all, I am a Tepanec. I should know. But maybe that's why they closed their ears."

She watched him, swept with compassion.

"No! That is not the reason," she said firmly, peering into his eyes, now dark and disappointingly guarded. "Our people value your opinions. They have been following you for more than a few summers. They trust you wholeheartedly. Believe me! I would know." She shrugged. "It's just that they didn't want to side with the Lowlanders. The Tepanecs are a distant threat, not known to us at all, while the Acolhua scum have been our sworn enemy for many spans of seasons. Why should we help them against an unknown menace?"

"Because the Tepanecs will prove to be worse."

"Oh, we know that. You and I, we know those people. But how many Highlanders have met a Tepanec in their entire life?"

His eyes twinkled as he grinned reluctantly. "All the people who have met me."

"No," she said, taking a firmer hold on his arms. "You are a Highlander. For more than thirty summers you've been the perfect Highlander, the warrior and the leader. The best leader my people could have asked for."

His smile widened, then deepened. "I wish our guests would go away."

"They will." She caressed his arm once again, smiling into his eyes. "By the time I come back, they'll be gone and we'll be alone, like when we first came here, all those summers ago."

His gaze dwelt on her, glimmering, reflecting, telling her that he remembered those times, when they were young and full of love, without a care in the world, coming to her woods and living there for moons, not bothering to look for a town to settle in, living off what nature had to offer them, making love for days on end.

"Hurry back," he said finally. "Don't let your duties come between us tonight."

She smiled. "Tomorrow there are no rites, and hopefully nothing urgent to solve. We'll have a whole day to ourselves."

"I'll have to call the council of the Clan Leaders, but I suppose it'll take them a few blissful dawns to organize." He shrugged. "I wish they would listen to me more readily. They'll come to know the Tepanecs soon enough if the Lowlanders go down, and it looks like they will." His face darkened once again. "I had word from my brother. The Aztecs will side with the Tepanecs now that Huitzilihuitl, their Emperor, is dead. They'll come here in force, too."

Her stomach turned once again, but she managed to keep her fears down this time. "I told you, not many Highlanders have met Tepanecs. But they will listen to you all the same."

He raised his eyebrows, then shrugged.

Before turning to walk back toward the patio, she saw his lips quivering, one corner of his mouth lifting into a mirthless grin. "I know of one Highlander who should know the Tepanecs quite well by now. Maybe he could come home and help me convince our people, unless he is approaching those shores with the Tepanec fleet of canoes at these very moments."

Her heart squeezed again. "No," she said. "He wouldn't do that. He is busy doing something else."

He refused to meet her gaze. "Alive?"

"Yes, I would know if he was not."

"Good. That's a relief." He glanced at her fleetingly, his grin forced. "I hope you are right about the rest of it as well. I hope he is not fighting with our enemies, side by side."

CHAPTER 2

The Lowlands, Coatlinchan
1418

"Oh, I hate the Aztecs," exclaimed Coyotl, his eyes blazing, fists clenched. "Cowardly, filthy, stinking dung-eaters, each and every one of them!"

Kuini could not suppress his grin. They were nearing the outskirts of Coatlinchan, leading a part of their warriors' forces, approximately one hundred men, because an unknown fleet was reported to be approaching the southern shores of the Great Lake.

The main battle was supposed to be raging at these very moments to the north of Texcoco itself, and Kuini knew how desperately his friend wanted to be there, in the middle of the action. Yet, here they were, sent away to defend the meaningless town of Coatlinchan from whomever wanted to attack it.

Whose fleet was it? he wondered, hastening his step, trying to keep up with the agitated heir to the Texcoco throne. So many nations had joined the Tepanecs this time, willingly or reluctantly. More and more of the fence-sitters of the previous two summers had decided to throw their fate in with the mighty Tepanecs. Even the dwellers of Lake Chalco, with all the old Tepanec warfare against it notwithstanding. Kuini shrugged. After two summers of living among the Lowlanders, of fighting with them side by side, he was still unable to understand them, not entirely.

And then, there were the Aztecs, of course. Oh, those managed to surprise even the Texcocans themselves. The arch fence-sitters, after the death of their Emperor, they had openly declared for the Tepanecs, forsaking relationship of many summers with their Acolhua neighbors and allies.

How could they do this? wondered Kuini, puzzled. Acamapichtli, Tenochtitlan's First Emperor was raised in Texcoco. And this didn't even begin to describe the list of the citizens and rulers with mutual history and blood ties. Both *altepetls* had been friends for, oh, decades, trading, building, fighting alongside each other. Also, Huitzilihuitl's Second Wife was the Texcoco Emperor's First Daughter, given to the Aztec island in order to strengthen the ties between the two nations; to guard the relationship of two *altepetls* against exactly what was happening now.

The thought of *her* made his heartbeat accelerate, while his stomach began fluttering in a familiar way. Huitzilihuitl, her husband, had been dead for more than two seasons. She had no husband.

He clenched his teeth tight. Oh, but he should not be thinking of her. She was not real. She was a part of a dream; a part of those few strange days when his life had briefly taken too many wild turns, turning into a tale worthy of a mad storyteller.

Remembering those days, he sometimes would think that he had made it all up, or probably just dreamed it. Was his perfectly Chichimec father really a Tepanec? Was the powerful Aztec Warlord his uncle? Had the Acolhua Emperor's First Daughter, destined to be given to the Aztec Emperor, made love to him, giving him her virginity? Had they truly planned how they would go about kidnapping her, while dreaming of their life in the Highlands together?

No, this crazy market interval, two summers ago, must have been nothing but a wild dream. *A market interval!* He shut his eyes for a heartbeat, trying to banish the dull pain in his chest. She had not been angry with him for not coming back. She had just thought he had gotten it wrong. Oh gods!

"Have the scouts already reported back?" Coyotl's voice broke into his thoughts.

"No, but we are expecting them back any moment, Honorable

First Son," said the leader of their force. "We won't be entering this town without advance knowledge."

"Maybe you should send another party," muttered the heir to the Texcoco throne, glancing at the sky. "We want to finish those invaders before the nightfall."

The veteran warrior just shrugged. He was the leader of these forces and, evidently, he didn't like the necessity of consulting a youth of barely seventeen summers, Emperor's heir or not.

"If I was Tezozomoc, I wouldn't come here," said Kuini, mostly to take his thoughts off the Aztec Second Empress. "I would attack Huexotla. This town is perfect to launch an offensive against Texcoco."

"Well, it's good you are not Tezozomoc," grunted Coyotl, not amused.

"What I am trying to say," insisted Kuini, "is that your father should send a force there, to make sure Tezozomoc didn't arrive at the same conclusion. I don't think Huexotla is well defended."

The broad face of the warriors' leader twisted as if he had eaten something incredibly bitter. "Tepanecs are no gods. They are attacking the north, trying to reach Texcoco from *that* direction. They can't be everywhere at the same time."

"Unless they are faking this northern attack," muttered Kuini, knowing he should hold his tongue. He was not an emperor's heir.

"Oh, mighty Tezcatlipoca, please spare me the guidance of *calmecac* cubs!" exclaimed the veteran warrior, storming off.

"Well done!" chuckled Coyotl, watching the leader's headdress disappearing behind the curve of the road. "My father should appoint you to be his Chief Warlord, you know? And the Adviser, too." Elevated from his previous gloom, he thrust his elbow into Kuini's side. "I shall talk to him about it when we get back. Get ready to wear that heavy headdress. It's not easy to carry."

"With the quality of some of his leaders..." Kuini shrugged. "But seriously, could it not be possible? An attack on Huexotla? Why would they attack from the north, with no good roads and the difficult terrain?"

"Because they did it two summers ago, you brilliant leader.

They know the terrain well. They remember what mistakes they made. Of course they would attack from the same direction. Why would they venture into unknown lands after their blunders here back then?"

Kuini shrugged again. "It's not like they couldn't send scouts. They had moons to prepare this invasion." He shielded his eyes against the strong midday sun. "We should have done it too, if you ask me. The last summer, when we were running all over their side of the Great Lake. After that battle near Tollan, we should have sent out an army of scouts and then attacked Azcapotzalco from the hills. We could have taken them from there. With surprise and a little luck, maybe."

Coyotl's grin twisted, became unbearably smug. "They would not be surprised. Not after we beat them at Tollan. They expected us to roll toward Azcapotzalco as fast as our legs would carry us."

"Then we should have done just the opposite. That would surprise them and unsettle them, and our scouts would have time to find the best place from which to launch the attack."

This time, Coyotl laughed outright. "Slow down, warlord. You have too many ideas. Where do you get these from?"

Angered by his friend's open amusement, Kuini clenched his teeth. "I get these ideas because I think, and I listen, and I have eyes, too. That siege on Azcapotzalco was a joke. We just made fools of ourselves and then ran back to our side of the lake. So here we are, with the Tepanecs back again, full of energy and better prepared." He took a deep breath. "Your father should choose better leaders to lead his warriors and to plan his campaigns. People like that Aztec Warlord, for example. He should have persuaded this man to lead his forces instead of trying to kill him time after time."

"Oh gods!" cried out Coyotl, enraged now as well. "You are talking so much nonsense, my head hurts. Do you listen to yourself? That Aztec Warlord was the dirtiest dung-eater I'd ever met, and he is probably leading his own warriors toward our shores in these very moments. Or maybe he is already there, fighting our people to the north of Texcoco." Whirling, he peered at Kuini, his lips pursed, eyes blazing. "What's wrong with you?

Has this southern road brought up too many memories, eh? Making you want to run from our warriors again, dragging after that dirty Aztec? Why don't you go and join him if you miss him so much? Such a precious brilliant leader who would know how to conquer Azcapotzalco itself."

Kuini stared at the glowing face, the flashing eyes, the thinly clasped lips. The urge to punch it grew. He clenched his fists tight, willing his palms to stop trembling. Coyotl was under much strain recently, put out most of the time, erupting at the slightest of provocations. But then, who could blame him? If the Tepanecs were forcing their way up his, Kuini's, mountains, nearing Huexotzinco maybe, as unstoppable as a lethal whirlwind, with other nations, old allies and friends, reinforcing the enemy, helping with relish, oh, in that case he might have been feeling as edgy and worse.

"Forget it," he said as calmly as he could. "You are the one talking nonsense now."

They reached the top of the hill and stopped, surprised. Coatlinchan spread ahead, sleepy and quiet, peaceful in the haze of the midday heat.

The warriors congregated all around, wandering the hill, conversing quietly. Close to a hundred men, dusty and sweat covered, warriors that should have been back in Texcoco, fighting the Tepanecs. What a waste of time and energy!

"What, in the name of the Underworld..." The rest of Coyotl's tirade trailed off as he rushed away to converse with the leaders.

Still seething, Kuini did not follow. The memories had, indeed, begun haunting him as they neared that sleepy town. Had it happened only two summers ago? He remembered nearing this same hill, just a youth of fifteen, ruffled by the wild days spent in Texcoco, anxious to get back to his mountains, his family, the normal way of life, yet still fascinated with the Lowlands, and most of all, with that formidable Aztec leader.

Oh, but did he remember that man well, so tall and imposing, dangerous, arrogant, but decent nevertheless, reliable and straightforward, a good man, a trustworthy person. *His uncle.* Oh gods, how ridiculous. He still couldn't think of the Aztec Warlord in those terms, couldn't bring himself to share this information with Coyotl.

He sighed. So much had changed since. He hadn't returned home back then, if one didn't count the short span of time spent in his father's house, recuperating. A few days to recover from his wounds and to try to cope with the avalanche of the family secrets. He had left still angry, with his father most of all.

He shrugged, perturbed by the old confusion, for now here he was, already a man, a seasoned warrior, a youth of seventeen, but with the experience of one twenty summers or more. He had seen more places than he could count, fought more battles and skirmishes than he could recall. Well, no, he could still recall every battle. Such a thrilling experience, although, sacking towns was not that pleasant.

Shivering, he remembered burning houses, shattered buildings, people running, and screaming, and dying, not only warriors but all sorts of people, with women taken brutally or tied to poles, led to the slave markets along with surviving men and children. He had managed to hang onto his stomach contents on such occasions, not letting the sense of disgust overtake him, but those were memories he preferred to forget.

Forcing his thoughts back to this side of the Great Lake, he sighed. Was the Aztec Warlord approaching their shores now? The man had promised it wouldn't happen. He'd said the Aztecs would never join their Texcoco enemies more than as a token war party or two, to keep the Tepanecs happy. Yet, now here they were, doing just that, attacking Texcoco with relish, invading those shores happily and with no reserve.

He suppressed the grimness of his grin, shaking his head against the confusion. It would be good to meet the Aztec now; to show him what kind of a warrior he, Kuini, had become. Still, he wished they would meet under different circumstances. Not on a battlefield, facing each other.

"We sent a group of warriors in," reported Coyotl, coming back. "To take a look and see what's happening. If it was a false message, we'll go back in a hurry. Maybe we'll still reach the battle in time to join."

"Exhausted, hungry, and spent," muttered Kuini, forcing a grin. "We'll be of a great help, oh yes. Although I'm sure they'll appreciate us all the same."

Coyotl made a face, back to his old cheerful self. "Oh, stop trying to anger me again. I'm frustrated as it is, without you making so many smart remarks in one day."

The sky was alight, blazing with different shades of yellow and orange, beautiful to look at against the deepening darkness. It spread to their east, but the vicious glow could be spotted in the greater distance, blazing at the north as well.

Speechless, they stared at it for a heartbeat, then broke into a heedless run, careless of the path, crashing through the bushes adorning the low hill. Huexotla was on fire! But how was it possible? thought Kuini, forgetting his own morning observations. Wasn't the fight supposed to be raging to the north of Texcoco?

His dread welling, heart pounding, he rushed on along with the rest of their warriors, heedless of prudence or any sort of the imminent danger. Whoever had set Huexotla on fire had clearly not tried to do it by surprise. Oh, no! The attackers of that southern town were surer of themselves than that.

Slipping along the alleys, their pavement awash with blood, stumbling over sprawling bodies, they stormed the outskirts of the large settlement, their swords and clubs ready, nerves taut. The Tepanecs seemed to be not too many, the brilliant-blue of their elite forces leaping dangerously into one's view every now and then, forcing one to concentrate, to summon one's strength and skill. The rest were just warriors, some foreigners, Nahuatl-speakers from all over the Great Lake.

Even though exhausted and hungry, a hundred Acolhua warriors were more than a match for the mixed enemy forces. The swords swished, the clubs rose and fell, the spears thrust. Arrows and darts flew by, shot from the rooftops, mainly by the enemy, although some defenders were still alive, with the remnants of their fighting spirits intact.

Yet, something was wrong here, sensed Kuini, a part of his mind refusing to give in to the battle frenzy, contemplating frantically. The Tepanecs were too few, too low-spirited to be the ones who had taken this town. No, their main forces had to be elsewhere.

Locking his sword with a bulky warrior, Kuini refused to think about those other forces and where they could have been now. No, not in the north, pounded his heart as he disengaged, leaping aside, trying to bring his sword toward his opponent's momentarily exposed side with the same movement. No, they could not have been in the north. The bulk of the enemy warriors must have been here in the south, rolling toward Texcoco, reaching the great *altepetl* from this unexpected direction, using the comfortable roads and the favorable terrain, washing over the southern neighborhoods, with their defenders located elsewhere, fighting their meaningless skirmishes in the north.

Glancing around, he sought out Coyotl, his heart beating fast. They had to take their warriors toward Texcoco, and they had to hurry. Racing past the ruined patios and gardens, past partly shattered gates and soot covered walls, he made sure to keep close to those, to press deeper into their shadows, to avoid the shooters of the rooftops.

The leader of their force was nowhere in sight, but he recognized one of the man's aides directing some of the warriors past a burning cluster of houses.

"Where is the First Son?" he demanded, squinting against the raging flames, fighting the urge to move away from the scorching heat that emanated from those.

The man turned around, startled. Narrowing his eyes, he peered at Kuini through the choking dusk. "I think he is with the warriors on the central plaza."

"Are you going there now?"

The man shrugged.

"He'll be taking his warriors to Texcoco." Kuini coughed, fighting the intensified urge to leap aside as a new gust showered them with a cloud of glowing embers. Satisfied, he saw the veteran warrior backing away. "You better bring your people to the plaza as well."

The man scowled, his eyes nothing but narrow slits in the muddiness of his soot-covered face. "Move on, warrior," he said, stifling a cough. "Either join us or run along."

Arrogant dung-eater, thought Kuini, rushing on, following the alley that to his reckoning must be leading toward the central plaza. Hearing the swish of a club, he ducked out of instinct, so the heavily weighted tip crushed against the plastered wall. His own sword reacted as readily, while his legs made him leap aside, to avoid another better directed blow. For a heartbeat, they stared at each other, his rival a tall, broadly built man, a typical Tepanec, his face glaring out of the fire-lit darkness.

"You are a Tepanec, aren't you?" breathed the man, thrusting his club toward Kuini's ribs.

"No, I am not." Bumping his back against the stone wall, Kuini managed to avoid the crushing touch of the heavy weaponry.

"Why do you fight with the Acolhua scum?" The man brought his club up, blocking the thrust of Kuini's sword.

Pressing with all his might, Kuini did not waste his energy on maintaining the conversation, his hands trembling, muscles strained, feeling as if they were about to burst. The wall behind his back would not let him disengage safely.

The pressure of the club grew. "You should fight with your people." His opponent's eyes glowed dangerously, so close he could feel the warmth of the massive body, could smell the stench of sweat, the *octli* on the man's breath.

He gritted his teeth, and with the last of his strength kicked at his rival's shin, slipping downward, letting the club crash against the wall where his back had warmed the uneven surface. The obsidian spikes of his own sword brushed against the man's skin, as he hurled himself past his opponent's legs and into the darkness of the street.

Ready to meet the new onslaught, he sprang to his feet, clutching the sword with both hands. His rival did not make him wait. Clearly enraged and not spending his time on any more talking, he attacked wildly, relentlessly. Yet, now Kuini had enough space to maneuver. Darting aside, he brought his sword down on the man's momentarily exposed back, but it landed flatly, sending the warrior reeling, not cutting his skin. Rushing forward, Kuini tried to catch the momentum, but his next hurried blow was blocked, parried by the heavy club.

The Tepanec's eyes glittered against the glow of the fire spreading up the narrow alley. He pressed again, but this time didn't seem to use all of his immense power to push his rival down. He was afraid of getting kicked, guessed Kuini, momentarily pleased.

Disengaging suddenly, this time he swayed backwards as if giving way under the pressure. The man did not waver, but his attention seemed to shift for a heartbeat, enough for Kuini's sword to make it upwards toward his opponent's lower belly.

It was not a good blow. The obsidian cut some flesh, but not deeply. Still, it made the man waver. Clutching his stomach with his left hand, the warrior's right palm still gripped the club, ready to fight; yet, with the continued bleeding, the Tepanec's fighting prowess seemed to deteriorate. A better directed thrust sent the man crashing against the wall. Still, he stood there, refusing to fall, stifling a groan, his breath coming in gasps.

"You chose your side stupidly," he hissed. "Acolhua excrement-eaters have already lost."

Kuini fought for his own breath, sword ready, curiously reluctant to finish the man off. "No, they have not."

"Our people have taken Texcoco... at high noon." The man coughed, slipping against the wall, still clutching his club.

"From the south?"

"Oh, yes. Your people were stupid enough to fall for the most basic trick in warfare history." The voice trailed off, weakening along with the warrior's life forces.

Kuini took a deep breath, trying to calm his heartbeat. "We'll get it back."

"With what?" The man coughed again. This time a dark flow trickled down his chin. "The stupid Acolhua warriors in the north are finished." He took a convulsive breath, tried to spit the blood out. "Your emperor is dead. He tried to get away and was hunted down by the Chalcoan warriors." The clouded eyes narrowed, as if trying to see Kuini more clearly. "And you are a Tepanec, anyway. A stupid Tepanec who has chosen the wrong side."

Loud footsteps echoed down the alley, and Kuini whirled to see more silhouettes rushing toward them, either their or the enemy warriors. Looking around wildly, he did not waste any more time on watching his dying opponent, but sprinted up the dark alley, his heart pounding in his ears. *Coyotl! He had to find Coyotl, and quickly.*

The small provincial plaza was ablaze, as bright as in daylight. He saw the Acolhua warriors congregating beside a high wall.

"Where have you been?" cried out Coyotl, grabbing his shoulder, pulling him into the protective darkness under the wall. "The slingers are shooting wherever they see someone. See? There, up on that temple's roof." The palm around his shoulder tightened. "You had me worried. I thought you were dead."

"No, not yet," gasped Kuini, still out of breath. "But it was close enough." He straightened up. "Listen, I heard some news. Bad news. They may be invading Texcoco from the south. In these very moments." To take his eyes away was tempting. "They say… they say it was just a diversion in the north. And also…"

No, he could not bring himself to say that. It may not be true anyway, and Coyotl did not deserve to receive this kind of news.

The tightened jaw of his friend shook for a moment, then the large teeth came out, sank into the taut lower lip.

"It doesn't matter," declared Coyotl finally. "My father's forces in the north will trap them in the city. And we will close on them from the other side." He straightened up resolutely. "We rally our warriors here, and then we move out in a hurry."

Kuini looked around, his stomach tightening. "We have hardly a third of our warriors here. The rest are gods-know-where, scattered or killed. Where is the leader?"

The dark gaze was his answer.

"There was one of the minor leaders with about ten warriors. I told him to come here to the plaza, but the stupid frog-eater didn't like receiving directions from me. Want me to run there and get his men?"

As Coyotl opened his mouth to answer, a swarm of Tepanecs poured onto the square. Swords and clubs grasped firmly in their hands, they halted and waved toward the temple and no darts or arrows came.

Kuini heard his friend cursing softly. No, they would not reach Texcoco tonight. The warriors by his side shifted their weapons, listening to the leaders, tense and surprisingly calm.

He watched them moving out slowly, like in a dream, their silhouettes blurry against the raging flames. His mind hollow, empty of thoughts, he followed. *So that was that? These two glorious summers, traveling the world, fighting battles, conquering, dauntless and invincible, would it all end up here, in this stupid gods-forsaken Huexotla?*

He felt Coyotl's arm gripping his shoulder.

"We stay close. Keep each other safe." The Texcocan's eyes flashed at him, suddenly light and unconcerned. "It's nothing to worry about."

Kuini's stomach twisted. "I have to tell you something—"

"More bad news? Save your breath. We are going to beat this lot and then we re-conquer Texcoco. You just wait and see."

The sensation of being in a dream did not disperse as the fight progressed, strangely blurry. Everything was slow, distant and surreal, as Kuini hacked his sword on and on, until his arms felt almost too heavy to lift. By that time, they were on the outskirts of the town, but he didn't know how they got there. There were still about half a twenty of their warriors with them, and Coyotl's head was bleeding, but he seemed well enough otherwise. Kuini's limbs were also sticky with blood, but most of it seemed to be someone else's, so he paid it no attention.

He turned his head only once, to catch a glimpse of Huexotla blazing behind their backs. There were so many people on the roads, running and screaming, wounded warriors, men and women, some clutching their children. And they were all talking at once, wailing, waving their hands, panic-stricken. He tried to make sense of it.

"We are off for Texcoco," Coyotl was saying.

"No. The warriors in the north are defeated. The Emperor is dead." He heard someone talking, and it took him quite an effort to realize he was the one who had said it.

"What?"

"Those people," he said, trying to force his mind into working. "They are not fleeing from Huexotla. They are coming from the north."

And then Coyotl rushed off, and Kuini thought his friend would not return, but somehow, the Texcocan was back shortly thereafter. Oh, he had only gone off to talk to the refugees, he realized.

"How did you know? How long have you known?" Coyotl's voice was low, difficult to recognize.

"There was this warrior I killed. I tried to tell you on the plaza."

He watched his friend standing there, in the middle of the road, amidst the desolated flow of people, legs wide apart, eyes blazing. Then the light went out of his eyes. Just like that. As though a gust of wind came and blew a torch out.

"So it's over, isn't it?" Shoulders sagging, Coyotl made an uncertain movement.

Unable to think of anything to say, Kuini just shrugged, ready to catch his friend should he start falling. Even in the flickering darkness, he could see how pale the familiar face had turned.

"So what now?"

And then, he knew it.

"Come," he said resolutely, catching Coyotl's arm and turning in the direction opposite to the current of people. "Let's go."

Coyotl did not resist, and they made their way silently, turning away from the road, pushing their way uphill.

"Where are we going?" inquired Coyotl after a while, voice low but firm.

"Huexotzinco. We are going to the Highlands. And we will stay there until you get your Texcoco back. We'll make my people help. They are great warriors, everyone knows it. They'll help you take it back from the Tepanecs, Texcoco and its five provinces."

It took Coyotl time to respond, but he didn't slow his pace, didn't try to change their direction.

"Oh well," he said finally. "But I want you to make it six. Six provinces. There were some areas to the north that never paid the tribute. When I'm the Emperor, I want to have it too."

Hard put not to laugh, Kuini felt his gloom lifting, dispersing, the dreamlike sensation disappearing for good.

"Oh, you greedy frog-eater," he cried out. "Next you'll be asking *my* people to pay you a tribute, eh? Forget it. Just forget it!"

CHAPTER 3

The Highlands, Huexotzinco
1419

Leisurely, Dehe made her way along the invisible trail, enjoying the early afternoon peacefulness, watching the patterns painted upon the dim forested ground. Sunrays, those that had managed to break through the thick foliage above her head, made the damp earth look spotted like the hide of a jaguar. A pretty sight.

Her light footsteps made no sound, and that pleased her as well. She could walk as quietly as any forest creature, and no one but animals and their spirits would be aware of her presence. Oh, yes, she knew her way around the forest, no one better. Especially the areas of her ruined village, her homeland, but she had grown to know Huexotzinco's forested mountains not badly. More so, since what had happened in the Sacred Grove two seasons ago.

Scowling, she remembered her confrontation with the main priestess, the scary old hag with unsettling yellow eyes and a bad temper. There was no sacrilege in what she, Dehe, had done. So she used the precious altar to respect her own Green-Skirt Goddess of her home valley. So what? Huexotzinco Obsidian Butterfly could use some flowers. The two goddesses were not rivals. However, the priests had been horrified, and the purification ceremonies went on for half a night; and since then, she had been an outcast, more alone than ever, avoided as if she had caught some easily spreading disease. Not that she minded any of that. She didn't need their company. Still, the winter was

long and full of gloom, and she could not get away from the
accursed town when it was freezing cold outside.

Never mind, she thought, shrugging. For now it was high
spring, and she could sleep outside and not have to go back to the
annoying town at all. And anyway, soon Huexotzinco would be
no more than a bad dream. Very soon! As soon as she gathered
enough courage to go away. Back to the other side of the Tlaxcala
Valley; back home.

She scowled again, displeased with herself. What was she
waiting for? She should have gone away summers ago. When the
people of her village, those who had managed to survive the
warriors, had headed for Huexotzinco, she was just a girl of
twelve summers, too small to be asked for her opinion or to be left
behind. Too small and too terrified. Even now, three summers
later, she would still break out in a cold sweat and her hands
would begin to tremble, her heart beating faster and faster until
her chest seemed as if about to explode, each time the terrible
memory would invade her mind or her dreams, relentless and full
of dreadful recollections.

Clasping her sweating palms tight, she shook her head,
banishing the terrible visions. Last autumn, when the annoying
priestess had banished her from the temple services, she had
almost welcomed this push to go away. But then the whole town
went into a frenzy over the news from the Lowlands. The
invading Tepanecs from the other side of the Great Lake had
defeated the Acolhua lowlifes so thoroughly, their emperor was
dead and their *altepetl,* along with its towns and provinces, had
been taken and sacked.

The news made the Huexotzinco people nervous, swaying
between the sense of glowing satisfaction at their erstwhile
enemy's humbling defeat and the concern for their own safety.
The Tepanecs were an unknown entity, but the War Leader of the
United Clans, who some said was a Tepanec himself, was
worried, and people did not tend to dismiss the opinions of the
renowned leader.

As a result, terrified of the thought concerning warriors' forces
that may be lurking around the Highlands, Dehe had stayed to

endure another winter of emptiness and gloom. But now it was warm and sunny again and soon Huexotzinco would be nothing but a bad memory.

When the muffled voices interrupted her peacefulness, causing her to halt abruptly, she could already smell the river, reaching her favorite cliff, about to enjoy its readily offered tranquility. Paces soundless, heart beating fast, she came closer, curious and very put out. Her favorite cliff was hers alone. No paths led to it, and no one would bother to climb it from the river side. Yet, now some strangers were conversing there, talking none of the pleasantly rolling tongues belonging the areas beyond Smoking Mountain.

Frowning, she tried to make sense of the foreign words. Not many people could understand the tongue of the Lowlands; less would be able to converse in it. Her curiosity aroused, she came closer, peeking from behind the cover of the thick tree. Unlike many people, she understood the tongue of the enemy. Her closest playmate from childhood had been a captive girl from one of the Acolhua provinces adopted into a village family, a clever girl of light disposition but with no gift of leaning tongues. It took her so long to learn the Chichimec words of her new people that Dehe picked enough phrases to converse with her friend in the Lowlanders' way.

"I understand my brother is not happy with what's happening." The man who said it sat upon the edge of the cliff, his back to her and the forest, his feet dangling free, not deterred by the height.

Dehe winced, recognizing the voice. The War Leader of Huexotzinco and the rest of the settlements. She had not mingled in the town's high circles, but the War Leader was not a man one wouldn't recognize or forget in a hurry. Also, his speech was slightly different, reminding Dehe of that same girlfriend from her childhood, and now, listening to the men speaking Nahuatl, she understood the origin of his peculiar accent better.

The other man, tall and springy, shrugged. "No. The former Chief Warlord is most definitely not happy, and there are many who share his sentiment."

For a while, silence prevailed. The War Leader leaned forward as if about to jump from the cliff.

"What is happening in Tenochtitlan is beyond my understanding," he said finally, his voice low, reflecting no emotion. "Their behavior in the Acolhua War was despicable."

The tall man shifted uneasily. "I can assure you, Honorable Leader, that many important, influential people do not agree with our *altepetl*'s current policies. Since our beloved Emperor, Revered Huitzilihuitl, left the world of the Fifth Sun, Tenochtitlan is in turmoil. Our current Emperor is just a child. He enjoys the wise guidance of his revered mother, yet the Empress is pure-blooded Tepanec, one of Tezozomoc's favorite daughters. Her understanding of Tenochtitlan's destination differ from that of the Mexica people. Hence the change in our policies."

"Huitzilihuitl was a relatively young man," commented the War Leader, still peering at the opposite cliff on the far side of the river.

The silence that followed was heavy, pregnant with meaning. Dehe hardly dared to breathe, clinging to the thick trunk with both hands, afraid that the thundering of her heart would give her presence away. She knew nothing, and cared even less, about the troubles of this distant, unknown Tenochtitlan, but what fascinated her was this obviously clandestine meeting of the mighty War Leader and some enemy from the Lowlands. Fancy speaking Nahuatl in the heart of the Highlands!

"So, the Tepanec Empress is ruling Tenochtitlan now," said the War Leader finally. "I can understand my brother's resentment. It's not what his much praised first Mexica Emperor, Acamapichtli, had struggled for."

His companion said nothing, but the man's back was rigid, and she could see his sweating palms clenching helplessly.

The Highlander war leader turned his head, measuring his foreign company with what seemed like a piercing gaze. Even from her safe distance, Dehe could feel the power the man's eyes radiated.

"What was my brother's message?"

The tall man tensed again. "The Honorable Warlord wishes to

make sure that all is well with you and your people." The narrowed eyes peered at the War Leader, conveying a message. "The Honorable Warlord trusts me entirely. He asked me to tell you that." A lighter shrug ensued. "Mainly, he wished to know how you get along with your new neighbors."

The leader's shoulders shook, but the laughter that came out sounded mirthless and grim. "Our new neighbors? Oh, they have been quiet so far, but it won't last. With the active support of Tenochtitlan, they may grow bolder as the time passes." He shook his head. "Not only the Tepanecs, but the Mexica warriors have been sniffing around the eastern shores of the Great Lake, now that Texcoco was given to them as a prize for their good behavior."

The foreigner winced. "Tenochtitlan benefits from its Acolhua province. It does nothing that your people wouldn't do given a chance."

"Tenochtitlan would benefit better having Acolhua people back as its allies, the way it has been for more than a few summers. Mexica people will not benefit from being absorbed into the mighty Tepanec Empire, even if it would improve their city's condition for a while."

Another silence descended, marring the clear afternoon air, making it heavier, more difficult to breathe. The next time he spoke the War Leader's voice was so low Dehe could hardly understand his words.

"If my brother and other influential people agree with me, tell them I may have a partial solution for them."

"What sort of solution?"

"The heir to the Texcoco throne is hiding here, in the Highlands."

The tall foreigner turned abruptly, staring at the War Leader, wide-eyed. "Netzahualcoyotl? The First Son of the Acolhua Emperor?"

"Yes."

"But it's impossible. How could he possibly hide here? He would be slain, sacrificed to your gods the moment he crossed the first pass."

The War Leader shrugged. "Nevertheless, he is here, in one piece and healthy, his spirit unbroken." He paused, then added, stressing every word. "Ready to be used should anyone think of a way to use him."

"How?" asked the man hoarsely. He cleared his throat. "In which way?"

The older man began to get up. "Talk to my brother and come back here. The Acolhua heir will wait until then."

As they turned to go, Dehe dove into the safety of the woods, her breath caught, heart thundering in her ears. She would be done for if caught eavesdropping on someone of so much importance. What had happened in the Sacred Grove two seasons ago would be nothing compared to this latest transgression of hers.

Coyotl bent above the carcass of a small deer, wiping his brow. *What, in the name of the underworld, do you do with this thing now?* he asked himself, finding it hard to suppress his joy.

He tagged at the arrow fluttering in the long-legged creature's side. It shook and refused to move, stuck deeply, too deeply. A good shot! He smiled broadly. Oh, he was a hunter, he was! And they'd be impressed, all of them. How could they not? It wasn't every day a man would go out, coming back with a deer, tracked and shot all by himself. Not even the oldest among Kuini's brothers, that hugely impressive warrior and a hunter with plenty of wives, the same man who looked at him, Coyotl, with his eyebrows raised demonstratively high. The annoying frog-eater. But now, even this formidable man would know that Coyotl was not a useless Lowlander with no sense or skill.

He wiped his brow once again, losing some of his high spirit at the thought of the work ahead. To impress them he would need to cut this thing, to bring only the good, useful parts of the game back to the town. He could not appear dragging the whole carcass along the broad streets of Huexotzinco. They would laugh about it for generations, curse their eyes. They thought so highly of themselves, those Highlanders, but here he was, shooting a deer, making it dead with one single arrow, even if from a ridiculously close range.

Putting his bow aside, he re-tied his hair as best as he could. His warrior's lock gave him no trouble, but the previously shaven parts of it grew wildly, sticking out, long enough to became a nuisance, but not enough to tie up comfortably. It was a pity these people did not trim their hair the way the civilized people did. After two seasons spent beyond the high ridges, this seemed to be his main complaint.

He shrugged, wiping his brow once again. His life was not truly bad, all things considered. The cold, rainless moons accompanied by the deepest of despondencies were over and it was a main thing. Oh, what harsh winters they had here in the Highlands. No wonder these people were tough. He shivered, remembering the cruel winds that would penetrate through the invisible cracks in the wooden walls, making the dwellings freezing cold at nights, when the fire would die out. He would stare at the fire, knowing that his life had ended, just ended, before having a chance to begin.

Yet, with the coming of spring he felt better. Kuini, relentless and uncompromising, had dragged him everywhere he went himself, whether just to gather firewood or to hunt and check on the traps. They would go with other people or alone, and the Highlander would explain everything to him, although with time, Coyotl discovered that Kuini was not a good hunter. His friend found no interest in dragging through the woods, he would remark, shrugging. It was the worst bore ever and the raised eyebrows of his town's folk made no difference to him. No more than the good-natured sneering of his numerous older brothers.

Coyotl grinned, somehow not surprised with this discovery. The Highlander did not fit with the life in Huexotzinco. That's why he had kept coming to Texcoco once upon a time. He was a born warrior, with a great potential to become a leader. Fascinated with great cities, sucked into the wars of the Lowlanders, Kuini hadn't been home since he was fifteen. But now, thanks to Coyotl and his trouble, he was stuck here, not entirely happy about it.

The complete opposite of his friend, Coyotl warmed to the life of the mountainous town once he got over his winter depression. He loved to wander through the woods, seeking tracks of the animals, alerted to the sounds all around him. He felt useful and efficient. He felt at peace.

So, with the passing of time, having learned more than a few words of the softly-rolling Highlanders' tongue, he began venturing outside on his own, without the guarding presence of his friend.

Kuini didn't seem to mind. From time to time the Highlander would disappear for days on end, heading down the maintains, to spy on the Lowlands, suspected Coyotl. He didn't want to know. He tried not to think of Texcoco. It was full of the Nahuatl spoken by Tepanecs now, crushing under the yoke of the Aztec tribute. Just another tributary in the multitude of other provinces all over the Great Lake. He didn't want to see his *altepetl* like that.

Pursing his lips, he returned his attention to the motionless carcass that was sprawling helplessly under his feet. It was not even bleeding anymore. Putting his bow aside and taking out his knife, he reached for the creature's neck resolutely. He had to start cutting somewhere.

"You do it all wrong."

The girl's voice made him jump. His heart thumping loudly, he stared at her, wild-eyed, taking in the soft curves of her body, outlined by the knee-length gown of softened hide, decorated with small pelts. Her hair sparkled, wet and free, glittering with drops of water, her eyes studying him somewhat dubiously.

"You killed this thing?" she asked.

Finding it difficult to understand her rapidly spoken words, he just nodded.

"Well, you are cutting it all wrong."

She came closer, her waist tiny, enhanced by a colorful girdle, thighs swaying, inviting inappropriate thoughts.

"Can't you speak?" she asked, raising her eyebrows. "I thought the dirty Acolhua enemies were smart enough to learn our tongue."

"I speak, I speak can," he said angrily, understanding the general gist, especially the words concerning dirty Acolhua enemies.

"Oh, that's good." She halted beside the carcass and studied it thoughtfully. "So, you shot a deer all by yourself. You must be very proud."

He winced at her open derisiveness. "I'm no proud," he said. "I shot it and it..." He searched for a word. "And it... mean no, nothing. I don't care."

Oh, how he hated his inability to express himself. He, who had studied oratory in *calmecac*, who could always speak with eloquence, the future emperor of Texcoco. He ground his teeth, thrown out of balance once again by the girl's dawning smile.

"Give me your knife," she said briskly, and when he did not move, she snatched the obsidian dagger from his hand in one decisive movement.

"See?" she said, kneeling beside his spoil. "You cut it here and here. That's the first thing." Unconcerned with her pretty dress, she leaned forward, reaching for the deer's shoulder bones. "You take those pieces out and you offer it to *Camaxtli*. He watches over hunters and not only warriors, you know?" Another fleeting, matter-of-fact glance. "Do you know how to make an offering?"

"No," he said, ill-at-ease. Her palms were small and pretty, but coarse, adorned by broken, uneven nails.

"You truly don't know anything, do you?" She offered him a juicy cut. "You take it with you, and you bring it to your home. They'll know what to do with it, but pay attention, so you will be able to do it all by yourself next time."

"Who are you?" he asked, taking the dripping piece of meat.

"I'm Iso," she said lightly, returning to her task, her hands holding the knife expertly.

"Iso only?"

"No, but I like it that way." Putting another neatly cut piece aside, she eyed the red juices running down her arms, dripping onto the rim of her dress. "Oh, curse it! I'll ruin my dress this way." As she glanced up, her eyebrows formed a straight line above her darkening eyes. "Are you going to stand there and watch me working all by myself?"

He knelt beside her, taking back the offered knife.

"I'll tell you what to cut and you do it," she said briskly, assuming the leadership. "But you give me two good cuts for helping you. It's nothing, considering the way you would ruin the whole thing without my help."

More amused now than angry, he let her direct him, aware of her nearness and some sort of delicious scent, something fresh and enticing, overcoming the heavy aroma of the fresh meat.

"You from here, Huexotzinco?" he asked. "I no see you before."

"No. I'm from the nearby village, though." She glanced at him. "I know who you are. I've seen you. Several times. It's not every day one gets to see an Acolhua Lowlander, so we came to watch you," she related after a thought, pushing her hair out of her face with the back of her palm. "Me and the rest of the girls. I saw an Acolhua captive once, but he was already cut, with his heart dripping on the altar at the Sacred Grove's temple of *Camaxtli*. He didn't look very impressive."

He shifted uneasily, then cursed as his dagger slipped, cutting his finger.

She giggled. "You are a lousy hunter, you know."

"You don't stay. You can go," he growled between his teeth. But it only made her burst into an outright laughter – a trilling, trickling sound.

"You have nothing to take these things in," she said after a while. "And me neither. I'll ruin my dress carrying my share of this meat."

"I go, call friend, my friend," he said, wiping his brow with the back of his hand. "You stay, keep an eye. Yes?"

Her face darkened. "Your friend is nothing but an annoying, dirty-minded piece of rotten meat. He is a lazy good-for-nothing, who knows only how to fight and do dirty things with girls." She tossed her head high. "I won't stay if he is coming."

"What?" Dumbfounded, Coyotl just stared. Kuini was anything but a dirty-minded warrior chasing girls. In fact, since Coyotl's coming here to the Highlands, he had never seen his friend looking at women. But for an incident with those notes sent to Iztac Ayotl, he might have assumed Kuini did not like girls at all. Not that his friend looked at young men, either. There were always a few warriors who liked to get pleasure with other warriors, but his friend seemed indifferent to that as well. No, she could not be talking about Kuini. He must have misunderstood her.

"Why are you staring at me like that?"

"My friend? He don't, don't do things you say."

"Oh, yes he does. Maybe he just doesn't brag about it." Her eyes flashed at him. "He laid with me once, promised to make me his woman, then disappeared, oh, for summers. Disgusting piece of rotten meat, that's what he is!"

He could not suppress a smile, thinking of Kuini fooling with this girl. A new facet to the fascinating Highlander.

"Well, then what we do? Who help carry meat?"

"Call for someone else."

"No one come help, not me. I... people don't like." He raised his eyebrows. "Acolhua dirty enemies, remember?"

She tossed her head high. "Well, maybe they don't like you, but they didn't kill you, so you have nothing to complain about."

Well, yes, he reflected. She was right on that score, and actually he was not complaining. The Highlanders treated him well, all things considered, and while there were those who would be disdainful or outright hostile, most residents of Huexotzinco, including Kuini's brothers, would regard him calmly, aloof and reserved but not inimical.

Surprisingly, he felt safe here beyond the mountains, and among these people, the fierce savages. He tried not to shake his head, finding it difficult to believe that he had thought about the Highlanders in such terms once upon a time. Oh, yes, one should definitely travel from time to time, even if under more favorable circumstances.

He thought of Kuini's brother, one of his brothers, at whose house they had been staying, enjoying this man's reserved hospitality. Kuini wouldn't stay at his father's house. Why? At first Coyotl had thought it was because of his father's status. The

War Leader of the United Clans should not harbor fugitives of the defeated enemy. However, in the course of the short winter moons, he had discovered that Kuini was the one opposed to it. He was angry with his father, that much was obvious. Distant and polite, but angry.

Well, Coyotl could relate to that, having heard his friend's story on their way from the burning Huexotla. The renowned Chichimec war leader turned out to be no Chichimec at all. Unbelievable! Still, he thought his friend might be overreacting. It was not like his father had done something shameful, had betrayed his people or gotten captured by the enemy. All Kuini's father had done was conceal his long-forgotten past. And anyway, the man looked like anything but a Tepanec. Actually, he looked like no people around the whole valley of the Great Lake. It was Kuini who looked like a Tepanec. But maybe this is why his friend was so angry, thought Coyotl, remembering how the Highlander had admired the mighty war leader as a boy.

"Well," the girl's voice broke into his reverie, "have you fallen asleep?'

He looked at her, so fresh and pleasing to the eye.

"You take meat, half. I take half. We carry like that." He brought his palms up. "No comfortable. But no choice."

She took it surprisingly well. "I can rub my dress with the root of *metl* to wash the stains off."

He imagined her crouching above a high river bank, washing her dress, wearing... what? The thought made him uncomfortable.

"What? Why are you staring at me like that?" she asked innocently, but her eyes glittered, telling him that she knew exactly what he'd been thinking.

"You go your village no trouble?"

"Oh, you would like to take me there?" The glint in her eyes deepened. "Well, you can't."

"Come meet tomorrow. Here," he said, suddenly weak with desire.

She regarded him soberly, her eyebrows high. "Maybe. Maybe I'll come. I'm not sure it's worth the trouble."

"It is!"

"Oh," her eyes clouded, lost some of their previous sell-assured spark, "it might be dangerous, for both of us."

"Why? Because I can't, can't take you be a woman?"

"Oh, no." She laughed lightly. "I don't need this. I already belong to a man. A great hunter and a good warrior. A much better man than this good-for-nothing friend of yours!"

He took an involuntary step back. "You belong man?"

Her laughter rang with its previous teasing superiority. "You get scared easily, Lowlander. My man has been away for days now. They went to see what's going on in your former lands, to take a good look at those annoying foreigners who threw your annoying people out of their stupid *altepetl*." Her smile beamed at him, unbearably smug. "So, come here tomorrow and wait. I may show up. One never knows."

Her paces were light, almost soundless on the damp forested ground, although she evidently had a hard time carrying the dripping meat in both hands.

CHAPTER 4

Fighting his impatience down, Kuini leaned against the edge of the cliff, gesturing to the others to keep quiet, pleased with their quick reactions. There were only five of them, just a few restless, curious youths from Huexotzinco, eager to know what was happening in the Lowlands. Not daring to venture too far, they had come down to the outskirts of Coatlinchan and lingered there for a few days, sniffing around.

Kuini wanted to make it all the way to Texcoco, but his companions could not gather enough courage for such an adventure. What they had seen in the Lowlands so far was enough to make them all uneasy, Kuini included.

No, it was not safe to wander about, not with the Tepanecs busy organizing their new provinces, sending hordes of warriors to secure their newly conquered villages and towns, to make the tribute collectors' task easier.

Kuini ground his teeth, thinking of Coatlinchan and Huexotla, and the beautiful Texcoco itself, glimmering in the soft afternoon light, spreading lazily at the foot of his favorite Tlaloc hill like an exquisite, carefully painted drawing upon the most expensive bark-paper. Just the way he had always remembered it, not from his adventures in the great *altepetl* but from his first sight of it as a child, a mere boy of ten summers, fascinated and enthralled.

Shaking his head, he concentrated on the trail down below. The group they had spotted earlier should have been crossing the narrow pass in those very moments, according to his calculations. A party of ten foreigners, Aztecs or Tepanecs, or maybe some of their newly acquired allies from Lake Chalco, who had evidently come to hunt here, on the outskirts of the Highlands. What cheek! And what stupidity.

Kuini grinned to himself, eyeing the narrow passage. They may have been only five youths, but in this mountain corridor they could take down thrice as many men, hunters or seasoned warriors. The stupid invaders should have known better than to venture into the Highlands, and he would be only too glad to teach them a lesson.

"Why aren't they coming?" whispered a youth beside him.

Kuini shrugged. "Maybe they stopped to rest or something. They'll come."

"What if we miss them?" asked another youth, shifting nervously. "I only have five good arrows."

"What could you possibly miss with five arrows?" growled Kuini, irritated. He glared at the rest of them. "Are you warriors or just stupid hunters?"

The first youth glared back at him. "Hunters are not stupid. You may boast about your time as a warrior all over Huexotzinco, but there is nothing wrong with being a hunter. I've been on raids with our people, and I've been hunting too. You can brag about your sword and all, but I'm better than you with a bow."

"Then why are you afraid you'll miss from such a close range?"

"I'm not afraid. I didn't say I'd miss. I just don't want you to think you can be our leader just because you have your stupid sword."

Kuini glowered at the youth, but the later refused to drop his gaze.

"Fine!" he said finally. "Let us disperse with these Tepanecs, then we'll see who is leading whom. Now keep quiet!"

He returned his gaze to the trail below, wishing the intruders would come out already. What was taking them so long? The opposite cliffs towered ahead, bright in the broad daylight.

He remembered entering this pass long, long time ago – three summers to be precise – leading the Aztec Warlord and his warriors back toward the Lowlanders' settlements. A battered, confused youth of fifteen. Oh, how uneasy he had felt entering this narrow corridor, sensing its danger, knowing that a good leader would not miss such an opportunity to trap the enemy. The opportunity that his father, being a great leader, hadn't missed of course. What had come next was so bizarre that he still didn't like to think about it. Yet, now here he was, poised on the *right* side of the trap, ready to use it.

Narrowing his eyes, he studied the trail once again, marveling at the clear visibility of their hiding place.

"Listen," he said. "We don't need all five of us shooting. There will only be ten of the excrement-eaters down there. So Soro and I will get down there and attack those who survive your arrows."

Soro, a tall youth of seventeen summers, nodded solemnly and said nothing. He was closest to what Kuini might have called a friend had he bothered with friendships. As children they used to play together, until Kuini became too absorbed with his frequent excursions to the Lowlands while still a boy, drawing away from his childhood playmates.

"Why you and Soro?" asked Koo, the first youth, suspiciously.

Kuini controlled his temper. "Because he has a club and I have a sword, and you three are better with bows. Does it make sense to you?"

"Well, yes," agreed Koo after another pause.

"You begin shooting when they near the middle of the trail. Don't use your bows the moment you see them appear or they'll just dive back where they came from." Kuini leaned forward. "But don't let them advance too far either, because then they could run behind those rocks." Oh, but he remembered those rocks and the great shelter they provided. Staring the glaring youth down, he turned abruptly. "Now you are in charge and this should make you happy. Soro, come."

Still seething, he leaped down the invisible path. Why did the damn frog-eater have to argue all the time? They had all come here following him, Kuini, so why couldn't this one just follow quietly, like the rest of them?

Gesturing for companion to stop, he listened, keeping very still. The wind swept dry leaves along the canyon's floor, the same way it had back then. Pushing the unpleasant memories away, Kuini concentrated on his senses. Ah, there. Muffled voices reached him, faint and too distant to try to understand their words. His heart leaped.

"Now," he whispered. "We are waiting for the boys to start shooting. So do exactly as I do. When you see me running out, follow, and strike any of those would-be-hunters, the ones who are still standing up. There should only be a few of them on their feet anyway, so just follow me, and don't think about anything else."

"I know what to do." Soro shrugged, giving Kuini a hard look. "Stop explaining it all to me. I've used a club before."

Kuini turned away, exasperated. "Oh, so now it's your turn to argue? Fine, do whatever you like!"

He concentrated on the trail just below their feet, another perfect vantage point. They should sit there constantly, he thought; waylay any intruders who might be trying to enter the Highlands. That would teach the Tepanecs to keep away. Not according to Father, but even the War Leader could be wrong from time to time.

The thought of his father made him uneasy. Since returning to Huexotzinco last autumn, after his absence of more than two summers, he had felt guilty, incredibly guilty. Father said nothing, demanding neither an apology nor explanation. Busy as always, he seemed uninterested in any closer contact, talking to his son politely and distantly when an occasion arose, but not trying to bridge the gap Kuini himself had created.

The man asked no questions and made no comments, accepting the request to shelter the heir to the Texcoco throne without a word, eyeing Coyotl with his eyebrows raised high, his gaze thoughtful, unreadable, flickering with humorless amusement. If there were such a combination.

Had the War Leader objected, Kuini knew, Coyotl would not have been accepted anywhere around here or in the vicinity of the Tlaxcala Valley. He would have been thrown out, or more likely, sacrificed on the altar of *Camaxtli*, the mighty god of the warriors and the hunters.

Kuini ground his teeth. If only Father were a little more approachable. However, with all his humorous disposition and lightness, the War Leader kept his thoughts to himself, and the way he had behaved with Kuini since his return, so distant and aloof yet cordial, indicated a deep offense. Oh gods, why was life so complicated at times?

He forced himself to concentrate on the trail in time for the Tepanecs to appear. Eyes straight ahead, the ten men walked tiredly, carrying their large leather bags, not sparing a glance to their surroundings, panting their way uphill.

How could warriors behave in that way? wondered Kuini, afraid to breathe, clinging to the crude surface of the rock, feeling its warm touch against his cheek. Yet, five of them were definitely warriors, their topknots prominent, their plain cotton cloaks swaying with every pace. Cotton, not maguey. The Tepanecs were so rich!

His relief vast at the discovery that the warriors' cloaks were nowhere near the shade of the brilliant blue, he shrugged. Five non-elite warriors. They should be able to handle those. He hoped Koo would have enough sense to aim at the warriors first, before trying to take down the people who carried the bags.

If only Coyotl were here, to fight alongside, the way they always did, guarding each other. Instead, he was stuck with four youths from his hometown, some of which were too busy arguing with him, trying to prove they were as good as him. Well, they weren't; of course they weren't!

The Tepanecs had reached the first part of the canyon and now were glancing around uneasily, understanding at least the potential of such a place. He remembered the Aztec Warlord being reluctant to even enter this pass, smelling a trap from a great distance. The man was a worthwhile leader, while the stupid invaders were beneath contempt.

The men approached the middle of the pass, but no arrows came. Kuini's palms went numb from the force with which he wrapped them around his sword's hilt. *Come on*, his mind thundered fervently, *start shooting*.

The people with the bags were so near he felt he could smell their sweat, and their fear. They hastened their steps, and some talked amongst each other quietly, glancing around. *Come on!*

Finally, the first arrow swished, and one of the men with the bags whirled, losing his balance and waving his hands in the air. Kuini exhaled loudly, straining his eyes, trying to see if the shot was any good.

Two more arrows flew, one missing its target, the other sticking neatly in one of the warriors. Kuini's heart jumped, but he caught Soro's arm, signaling that it was not the time to run out, not yet.

The people below their cliff moved around in confusion, and he could hear the warriors yelling, waving their arms, clearly urging the men with the bags to move quicker.

Kuini's chest tightened as if about to explode. No more arrows came, and he wanted to climb up and kill his companions one by one. Stupid frog-eaters!

He tossed his sword aside and snatched the bow that Soro bothered to drag along. It was a good, sturdy weapon, flexible and easy to manage. Pushing his friend unceremoniously, he reached for the bunch of arrows, pulling one out and not caring about the youth who had almost lost his balance, bumping against the cliff.

Hurriedly, he stretched the bowstring and was about to peek out, when Soro grabbed his shoulder. "You can't!"

Kuini shook the arm off, taking his aim hurriedly, knowing he had time for only one shot before they saw him. Not a good shooter, from such a short range he could not miss. The warrior nearest to him fell flat on his face, the colorful feathers fluttering, sticking out of the man's back.

"Give me another arrow," hissed Kuini, not trying to keep his voice down, not anymore. He could see their twisted sweat-covered faces turning in his direction, their eyes widening, filling with comprehension. The warriors' gazes sparkled, and two of them charged toward their cliff, their clubs high.

He snatched the arrow from Soro's trembling hands and tore at the bow string, not aiming at all. The missile flew harmlessly, bumping against the nearest cliff.

His heart thumping insanely, he leaped to his feet, snatching his sword up in time to divert the blow of the first clubman. The sturdy weapon slipped down his sword's wooden handle, and he felt the paralyzing pain as its heavily weighted tip collided with his arm.

Losing his balance, he stumbled, but the cliff behind him cut into his back, helping him not to fall. With an effort, he brought the sword up, parrying another attack. That warrior was good; and angry.

Holding out against the pressure, Kuini tried to kick at the man's legs, a tactic that always worked. Somehow, they all seemed to concentrate on the duel of arms. The warrior stumbled, and now Kuini was able to push him off with a violent shove.

Not pausing for breath, he attacked without looking, charging heedlessly, knowing that this way of fighting upset many adversaries. His opponent blocked the next thrust, yet his hands shook, and he gave way under the pressure, clearly unsettled with the necessity to fight on the defensive.

Sensing his enemy's indecisiveness, Kuini disengaged, bringing his sword up again, from another direction. This time the obsidian spikes bit into some flesh. He could feel his sword sliding down, tearing at something soft, his arms absorbing the sensation, enjoying it, his ears taking in the man's gasp, relishing the sound.

His nerves stretched, eyes having difficulty seeing, he pushed the man away with a violent thrust of his shoulder and felt the firm body offering no resistance this time. In another heartbeat, the warrior rolled down the low rocks, limbs stretching, still trying to grip onto something, his face twisted in agony.

Blinking the sweat away, Kuini looked around, anxious to catch his breath, trying to understand. Soro was pressed against another rock, his temple bleeding, his club nowhere to be seen. With his adversary bleeding too, it seemed the youth was not completely lost, still, Kuini leaped forward, the flat side of his sword crashing against the other warrior's topknot. The blow echoed eerily, bouncing against the boulders of the small ravine.

"You can finish him off if you like," he gasped, taking in his friend's shocked expression. "I'm off to see what's out there."

Out on the trail, arrows flew in disarray, falling around the dead and the wounded men. Kuini counted two warriors and two hunters. The rest were nowhere to be seen, either hiding behind the rocks or, more likely, rushing on down the pass.

He shrugged, then wiped his forehead, surprised to see his palm coming back glistening with blood. His elbow still pulsated with pain, yet, swollen and half numb, it seemed whole, so he must have been cut somewhere else.

"Stop shooting, you stupid half-wits," he yelled as another arrow swished by. He shielded his eyes against the glow of the high-noon sun. "Get down here."

At the sound of hurried footsteps, he whirled around, clutching his sword, wincing from the pain in his hurt arm. But it was only Soro, making his way hastily down the trail.

"Are you good?" panted the youth, blinking.

"Yes. You?"

"Oh, yes." He hesitated. "You said to finish this warrior off, but I didn't know if you meant it. I mean, wouldn't you want to take him alive?"

Kuini frowned, aware of the pain spreading above his forehead. "You must be joking," he said tiredly. "I can't take this man. He was your enemy." He shrugged. "And you can't take him either, because I interfered."

"I know, I know. I just thought..." Soro's voice trailed off as his gaze wandered around, undecided. "You fought so well," he added finally, straightening his gaze. "It was scary. At some point we stopped fighting and just watched you two."

"You did?" Kuini felt like laughing hysterically. "It was not a good fight. This man was good, and I hate fighting in closed places." He touched the top of his head once again, feeling out the warm stickiness. "I didn't even notice he got me somehow."

The others descended the rocks, approaching them slowly, guiltily. Kuini shot a dark glance at them and said nothing. They knew they had failed. He didn't need to tell them.

"So now what?" asked Koo, fussing with his bow.

Kuini shrugged. "So now nothing. We go home." He glanced around. "We take their clubs, though. And the bags of those two. And the cloaks." He grinned humorlessly. "Fancy coming hunting into our lands."

"They'll be thinking again before they come next time."

"With the success of our so-called ambush, I'm not so sure they'll be thinking that hard." Unwilling to drive his point home, he turned around and went to pick up the clubs.

The silence behind his back was heavy.

"Soro did fight with you, and we shot those two warriors," said Koo finally. "It's not like you did it all by yourself."

Struggling to untie the string that fastened the club to the dead warrior's girdle, Kuini did not bother to look back.

"I didn't say I did it all by myself. All I'm saying is that you messed the whole thing up." He straightened tiredly. "You should have been aiming at the warriors, and you should have been shooting one arrow after another. As it was, most of those frog-eaters got away, while we made complete fools of ourselves." Feeling empty, he went toward a nearby tree, ignoring their glares. "Forget it. Get the bags and the other club, and let's go home."

The tree was old and ugly, spreading its branches in ungraceful disarray. At the level of his eyes a large piece of a bark was missing, peeled off by an alarmingly tall far-reaching creature. A bear? A few diagonal cuts left by a vicious blow of sharp claws made Kuini think of a jaguar rather than a bear, standing on its back paws, half man and half beast.

Mesmerized, he stared at the smooth surface, seeing that jaguar clearly now. Just a few more lines, to make it clearer. His hand came out as if of its own accord, fingers fastening around the hilt of his dagger.

The razor-sharp obsidian cut the wood easily, leaving strong, definite lines. He could feel the heavy silence behind his back. His companions must have been watching, wary and afraid. He didn't care, suddenly needing to do this.

The thought of the Tepanecs passing by this tree just a little while ago made his knife move strongly, giving his cuts more depth. Two more strokes to enhance the strong jaw, and he studied the carved face, pleased with its pointed ears and its bared teeth. The creature, although crude and unfinished, was that of his vision, staring back, threatening, its eyes round and empty but more unsettling because of that. It would not welcome the passersby, locals or intruders alike.

It would show the Tepanecs, he thought, turning back, now calm and not angry, not anymore. The intruders were not welcome in these lands and he, Kuini the Jaguar, had made it clear now. They better not come here again.

Ignoring his companions stares, he pushed his way past them. "Are you going to stay here until nightfall?" he tossed over his shoulder, heading back toward the trail.

They reached Huexotzinco toward the late afternoon, walking gloomily, saying little. On the outskirts of the town Kuini left his followers, explaining nothing. He wanted to wash up and to be alone for a while, to think it all through.

The winter in his hometown was bad enough, but the spring made him restless beyond any reason. He didn't want to be here, in the tranquility of the mountains. The calmness of the woods frayed on his nerves. It was fake, unreal. Terrible things were happening all around the Great Lake and beyond it. The world as he knew it was changing, crashing down, and this island of peacefulness, his homeland, the place that had known no peace before, dismayed him, made his skin prickle.

This situation would not last, he knew. The Tepanecs would come, and if not them, then the Aztecs, busy plundering Texcoco in these very moments. Or maybe the Chalcoans. The Acolhua people were enemies, but they were known enemies, with certain rules and traditions concerning the warfare between the Highlands and the Lowlands. While the Tepanecs...

Who knew what those undoubtedly fierce people were capable of? If they had managed to throw the Acolhua Emperor off of his throne, taking his *altepetl*, his towns and provinces, then what was to stop them from conquering his, Kuini's, mountains all the way to the Tlaxcala Valley, taking its villages and towns, burning them? Their hunger for conquest knew no bounds, or so it seemed. They would not rest until the whole world had become their tributaries.

Scowling, he made his way up the riverbank, putting much distance between himself and the favorite swimming and resting places that the Huexotzinco people frequented. It was a pleasant afternoon, and he could bet ten cocoa beans that many people were out there, splashing and fooling around.

A good swim somewhere away from the people, he thought, and then he'd go home to look for Coyotl. After two seasons in the Highlands, the highborn heir to the Texcoco throne seemed perfectly absorbed in the life of the mountainous town, not needing Kuini's guidance and protection as badly as in the beginning. Still, given their exceptional circumstances, one could never be too careful. The enmity between their nations went back generations, too deep to trust his, Kuini's, peoples' hospitality and their sense of honor with no reservations.

A lone cliff ahead beckoned, offering much-longed-for solitude. His elbow still hurt, and his headache grew worse with every passing moment, still, he climbed the invisible trail, needing to be alone.

While offering his friend shelter here in the Highlands, he hadn't thought it all through. They had lost a battle, escaping with their lives and little else, having nowhere to go, watching the world burning around them. The Highlands seemed like their only option, but he didn't think they'd stay here, in the town of his childhood, doing nothing. Confused and at a loss, he remembered assuming that his father would organize his warriors and would lead them all the way down, to take Texcoco back from the Tepanecs. At the time, it had seemed like a good, sensible solution.

Grinning humorously, he reached the edge of the cliff, out of breath. How naïve! Coyotl was now a refugee, offered shelter and little else. A very grateful refugee, and even seemingly content. Was Coyotl planning to stay in Huexotzinco for good, turning into the perfect Highlander?

He ground his teeth, frustrated beyond reason. Whatever were his friend's preferences, he, Kuini, wouldn't stay here and wait for the world to collapse on its own. If no action was planned here in the Highlands, then he'd go elsewhere. To Tenochtitlan, maybe. He could go to the Mexica island and look the Aztec Warlord up. The man was his uncle, and he had offered to recruit Kuini into his warriors' forces three summers ago, when he was a mere youth with no experience. But now? Oh now, the man should be more than happy to have him.

Tenochtitlan, he thought, aware of the cavity growing inside his stomach, making it twist painfully, with much force. What happened to imperial wives upon their masters' death? Were they given away, kept in the Palace, or maybe returned to their homelands? He shivered. She had nowhere to return to now, so she must still be in Tenochtitlan.

Untying his sword, he studied it, making sure no obsidian spike felt loose. He always did this, replacing even the slightly cracked ones, more often than needed, and always by himself. He did not trust anyone to tend to his sword, even though the Lowland warriors were only too happy to make the commoners fix their weapons, eager to exchange those for newer ones given a chance.

His fingers slipped over the elaborate carvings that covered his sword's handle almost completely now. Shutting his eyes, he felt the deep cuts upon the polished wood, recalling most of the times when he had carved them, going away after each battle, needing this solitude to clear his mind, but also to commemorate the slain enemy, whether captured or simply killed. His sword's handle honored them all, a cut for each man he had bested in a fair hand-to-hand, each killing dedicated to mighty *Camaxtli*, the god of war, watching over warriors and not only hunters.

His eyes slid over the vacant surface of the polished blade, and suddenly, his dagger was out and his hand was carving, acting as though it had a mind of its own. Careful not to damage the obsidian spikes, he worked frantically, unable to stop. The figure of a man holding onto a symbolic club, leaning backwards, defeated, came out easily, recognizable or not, he didn't care. However, the image of the attacker with a sword and the head of a jaguar was more difficult to create.

Teeth locked around his lower lip, he worked frantically, carving on, adding decisive lines, wholly immersed, needing to finish, needing to have this engraving upon his sword badly now. Not like the symbolic lines on the handle of his sword, but the exact depiction of this morning's hand-to-hand with the fierce Tepanec, the warrior who had been difficult to defeat.

Critically, he studied the engraving, adding an occasional line, correcting the angles until the attacking jaguar looked perfectly real, making his stomach flutter, reliving those glorious moments when his heart would pump insanely and he would yet again conquer the doubt and the fear, tottering on the brink but managing to avoid the heavy pull of the Underworld, besting another man, sending another worthy rival into the swirling mists of the afterlife instead.

Trembling with excitement, he took a deep breath, studying his work once again. The carving was good, real and alive, unpainted but vivid. Well, how could one paint a carving on one's sword? The colors would come off with the next battle, washed with the blood of the enemy or cleaned by the cotton cloth that the warriors cleaned their swords with.

Suddenly he caught his breath, the disturbing sensation creeping in, making his stomach tighten. No leaf moved and no branch cracked, still, his skin prickled and his nerves tensed like overstretched bow strings, letting him know that he has been watched.

Sliding slowly and carefully, his fingers tightened around the hilt of his dagger, leaving the sword to rest where it was. If he needed to move fast, the dagger would serve him better, against a human or an animal alike. Unless it was a warrior!

He shivered, then turned around slowly, pulling his legs off the edge. The greenish wall glittered, glowing merrily in the late afternoon sun. He sat there motionless, ready to pounce, scanning the trees with his gaze, little by little. Nothing. He might have imagined it. Still, he got to his feet, breathing deeply, trying to calm his heartbeat.

Studying the green foliage once again, he listened intently. Not a sound. If it was an animal, it must have frozen or gone away on its padded soft paws, disturbing no leaf. He shivered, imagining the sinewy spotted legs.

Carefully, he took a step toward the trail, then hesitated. This time the foliage rustled lightly and urgently, although there was no breeze. No, it was no animal. Only a human would move at the same time he started to move. Another heartbeat of hesitation. This time his eyes picked up on a slight movement.

His instincts deciding for him, he let his legs take him forward in one long, sudden leap, diving between the densely poised trunks, his sweaty palm clutching the dagger, the carved handle cutting into his skin.

Feeling the movement more than seeing it, his eyes finding it difficult to adjust to the dimness of the thick grove, he charged toward it, ready to evade a blow, ears tuned to the hissing sound of a possible shooting. The slender silhouette slid away, disappearing between the thick trees.

Jumping over fallen logs, he rushed after it, still in panic, his heart pumping insanely, senses in turmoil, tuned in to the sounds and the movement ahead of him, registering nothing else. Closing the distance, he doubled his efforts, miraculously not stumbling over the fallen logs and the slippery, moss-covered ground.

The fleeing figure tripped, skidded on the damp rocks. Struggling to get back onto her feet, she twisted like a snake, half leaping, half crawling away. However, before she managed to regain an upward position, Kuini was upon her, grabbing her shoulder, turning her around forcefully, needing to know.

A glimpse of a small terrified face rewarded him, before the girl twisted out of his grip. Swaying, she regained her balance, leaping backwards, charging for the nearby cluster of trees.

Out of an instinct, he grabbed the rim of her blouse, feeling the light material tearing, but still she struggled to break free, oblivious to anything but getting away, slipping upon the muddy ground and losing her balance once again.

"Stop it," he gasped. "Stop fighting me. I won't hurt you."

Her eyes were enormous, almost round, gaping at him out of the paleness of her face, beyond any normal state of fright. Now, as his nerves began to calm down, he could see that she was just a girl, very young and very terrified, sprawling there in the mud, clearly afraid even to breathe, staring at him the way a person would stare at the poisonous snake or the nearing jaguar, not daring to make a sudden movement, or maybe just paralyzed with fear.

He took a deep breath, trying to calm his heartbeat.

"Get up," he said, taking a step back. "And stop looking so scared. I won't hurt you."

She still gaped at him, her eyes round and as if glassed, her face lacking in color, like that of a sick person. He busied himself tying his dagger back in place.

"If I go, will it help you to come back to your senses?" Her terrified face reminded him the sacked towns on the other side of the Great Lake. Not an uplifting memory.

Dagger tied safely in its place, he found nothing else to fiddle with.

"Oh well, I'm going," he said, turning around. "But you were the one to spy on me. I wouldn't have gone after you if I'd known that you were just a girl." He shrugged. "Sorry I scared you."

"Why are you talking in our tongue?" Her voice reached him but barely, as he went back toward the light of the clearing.

"What?" He turned around abruptly.

The girl was sitting now, hugging her knees protectively, still tense and ready to flee. Or to go back to her terrified state. Her huge, oval eyes measured him warily. "Who are you?" she asked finally. "What are you doing all alone so near Huexotzinco?"

He stared at her, perplexed. "I live here."

Now it was her turn to open her eyes wide.

He frowned, unable to make sense of it. "Who did you think I was?"

She measured him with another wary glance, then dropped her gaze. "A Lowlander warrior," she muttered.

He felt like laughing, but not in a merry way. "I've been taken for a Tepanec, but for an Acolhua Lowlander?" He shook his head. "You are really not that bright, are you? Where are you from?"

She frowned. "You look like a Lowlander, and you had this

sword. I'm not stupid. Only Lowlanders are fighting with swords."

His heart missed a beat and without another word he dashed back toward the cliff, remembering the sword. To his imminent relief, it was still there, where he had left it needlessly, and without thinking. He clasped his lips tight. How reckless, stupid and reckless!

The girl stood at the edge of the clearing, watching him. In the soft light of the afternoon sun she looked younger, a cute little thing, thin and angular, too small for the wild mass of hair that cascaded down her shoulders all the way to her tiny waist. With her torn gown and this disheveled, unruly hair she looked like a wild spirit of the woods.

"Who are you?" he asked, having finished tying his sword.

She kept silent as her oval eyes studied him carefully, still wary and suspicious. He turned away and watched the river, remembering his earlier resolution to wash up and go looking for Coyotl.

"I thought you were a warrior," she said haltingly. "That's the only reason I spied on you. I wanted to know if you were alone, before going to the town to notify people."

"You are not from Huexotzinco," he said, shrugging, not amused at being taken for a Tepanec, or any other sort of a Lowlander, once again.

"Yes, I am."

He snorted. "Do you still take me for a stupid Lowlander? I grew up in this town. I would know. You talk with an accent, and you dress differently." He measured her with a pointed glance. "Not to mention your looks."

She frowned and her forehead creased, her eyebrows creating a single line above her darkening eyes. "I live here now," she said forcefully. "Well, I have lived here for the past three summers, but I will go away soon."

"Where to?"

"The other side of the Tlaxcala Valley."

"A long way."

She lifted one shoulder briefly, and her face closed, emptied of any trace of liveliness.

He looked back at the river. "I have to go," he said, shrugging. "Sorry for scaring you like that."

"Are you going back to the town now?" She measured him with a glance, openly skeptical. "Looking like that?"

He was taken aback. "Looking like what?"

Her eyes slid over him, making him feel embarrassed. "Dirty, covered with mud and bleeding."

"I'm not bleeding, and I was going to wash up in the river."

She pointed at his head. "Your hair is full of dried blood."

"Oh." He grimaced, remembering the morning skirmish. What a stupid encounter it was!

"There is a brook down that trail. You can wash there, and I can look at your head and see if it's serious."

He glanced at her, puzzled. "You understand these things? You seem too young and too wild for that."

Her eyes flashed angrily. "I'm not too young, and I'm not wild. I know everything there is to know about herbs and treatment. I was trained by the best healer of our village." Her face darkened. "And I was trained to be a priestess over here, too."

"In the Sacred Grove?"

"Yes."

He could not hold his laughter anymore. "You are making this up. If you were trained to be a priestess, you would be in the Sacred Grove now, sweeping the temples and cleaning the altars. You wouldn't be running all over these woods, spying on people and talking nonsense."

"Oh, so you know everything, eh?" She stomped her foot, and the mass of her tangled hair jumped angrily. "I said I *was* trained to be a priestess. I'm not anymore."

"How does one stop one's training?"

She shrugged and dropped her gaze. "There were problems," she muttered. "The main priestess was difficult."

"The priestess of the Obsidian Butterfly Goddess?" He felt like laughing. "She is not that bad."

"She is a real hag!" The girl tossed her head. "She is a mean, bad-tempered, yellow-eyed witch."

He stared at her, perplexed. "Now you are truly not making any sense. I happen to know this woman. She is none of that." He shrugged. "She may be sharp and tough, but she is not mean, and she controls her temper better than anyone. She is a reasonable person. Trust me, I know her well."

"Apparently not that well," insisted the girl. "The Priestess may look reasonable, but she is not. And you don't want to cross her path when she is angry with you."

"I crossed her path twenty times and more, and she's been angry with me more times than you can count." He grinned at her puzzled face. "The Priestess of the Obsidian Butterfly Goddess is my mother."

The girl's eyes grew so large and round he thought they might pop out of their sockets. "It's not true," she breathed. "You are teasing me."

"No, I'm not." He fought his grin from spreading. "But don't worry. I won't be telling her any of that." She looked so small and dumbfounded. "I promise."

He watched her even, white teeth sinking into her lower lip. "Oh, I don't care!" she said finally. "You can tell her whatever you like. I won't stay here, anyway. I'll be away by the time she hears you."

Curiously unsettled, he saw her eyes hardening. It made her look older. And so did the grim lines that now ran alongside her pressed mouth.

"Back to your village?" he asked.

"My village does not exist anymore. It was sacked and burned to the ground. But there are plenty of other villages on the other side of the Tlaxcala Valley, and they are safe now that the Lowlanders are getting what they deserved."

Oh, that would explain her terrified state when she took him for a Lowlander, he thought randomly. "It's a long journey for a girl to make all alone."

"I can manage." She made a face. "I've lived here in the woods since the beginning of the last moon." Pondering her own words, she added, "since the frost had retreated." Her gaze stood his, challenging. "I would have done it earlier, right after the priestess had thrown me out, but it was not possible through the Cold Moons."

"I see." He shifted uneasily, wishing to go away, yet wishing to stay now as well. "If you need something let me know. I can get you things, meat and stuff."

Her eyes twinkled, and the corner of her mouth lifted in a reluctant grin. "You are a warrior. The only meat you can get me is of the enemy warriors."

He grinned back, liking the sight of her smile. "You may be surprised." He thought about the bags they had taken from the Tepanecs this morning. "We just brought plenty of meat into the town. Well, not plenty, but enough to make a feast."

"Oh, then you probably should go or you'll miss your feast." She shifted her weight from one foot to the other, then wrinkled her nose. "Although, you do need that wash up, the way you look and smell."

He hesitated, but only for a heartbeat. "Oh well, show me that brook of yours."

"You are not doing me any favors," she declared, turning around and diving back into the dimness of the grove. "I am the one doing you a favor. Especially if I bother to take a look at that head of yours."

CHAPTER 5

"I say we should raid the Lowlands the way we have done for twenty upon twenty of summers." The thin lips of the slight elder pressed tightly, as he gazed at the War Leader, his eyes squinted challengingly.

From her hiding place, Mino watched the leading men of Huexotzinco squatting in a circle around the fire, hardly visible in the strong afternoon light. They were all there, the leaders of the warriors, but the priests too; even the head of the town, with some heads of the clans from their settlement and the surrounding villages. Many people, many representatives, the best of their region.

The women beside her held their breath. No young girls were allowed to eavesdrops, but respectable matrons like her could do this by the unspoken agreement of the whole town. It had become a custom. A wise custom at that, she reflected, making herself comfortable against the warm rock.

She watched her husband straightening his shoulders. "Indeed, our Flowery Wars against the Lowlanders were always a good tradition, bringing our warriors much glory, keeping our settlements safe and our gods satisfied with plenty of sacrificial offerings. And yet," he turned his head, and she could see his proud, eagle-like profile as his sincere, forceful gaze encircled the listening people. "And yet, the situation in the Lowlands has changed. Our enemy is no longer capable of conducting the same sort of warfare, while a much stronger people have taken possession of their towns. To raid the Lowlands now may not be a wise course of action."

She could hear him pausing, encircling them with another one of his piercing gazes. He was giving his words time to sink in, she knew. He was a good orator, better than many.

"The Tepanecs who have defeated our lifelong enemy are strong and fierce. Yet, had they only been that, we would have been able to keep them at bay, using the tactics we have used against our Acolhua enemy. Alas, our new adversary holds another advantage. They are relentless, and their determination knows no bounds. They have the resources of the large empire to rely upon. To stand up to this new enemy, to battle them, to keep our settlements safe, we will need all our skill and experience, all our wisdom and caution. However, we will also have to change our tactics."

He paused once again, and her chest swelled with pride. How wise he was, how courageous, how eloquent.

A woman beside her, the Chief Wife of a council member, murmured something, shaking her head.

"What?" whispered Mino irritably.

"He talks well, however his words will fall on deaf ears this time," breathed the woman.

"Why?"

But her companion just motioned with her head, suggesting paying attention to the happenings below their rock.

"What do you suggest we do, Honorable Leader?" an elderly man, the head of one of the clans, was asking.

"For one, we will need to guard our passes. We will use our advantage of the familiar terrain by trapping any warriors' force that may try to venture into our lands. Yet, we'll be careful to do nothing to provoke the enemy. We will not venture into their new domain." She watched him raising his palm against the murmuring of his audience. "Yes, for some time we will have to war defensively. But this situation will not last. The Lowlanders made a mistake by provoking the Tepanecs. We will not be so foolish. We will avoid making the same mistake by all costs." He paused once again. "For some time we will have to do that, however this situation won't last. The Tepanec Empire has swallowed up too many lands. They will not be able to hold onto their new possessions. Too many nations are unhappy, struggling against the foreign domination and the heavy tribute. United, they have a chance of throwing this dangerous enemy back into the Great Lake."

The deep silence prevailed, letting the sounds of the forest all around them to burst unrestrained, the calming rustling of the trees, the creaking their branches, the trickling of a nearby brook.

He was right, this man of hers, reflected Mino, not daring to shift in order to make herself more comfortable. The Tepanecs seemed to be invincible, but by playing in a wise fashion, by being careful, the Highlands might have a good chance of surviving, still proud, still independent, as they'd always been. While, if united with some of the conquered, subdued, or swallowed nations…

"With all due respect for the opinion of our War Leader," said Ai, the man who had suggested raiding the Lowlands in the first place. "I beg to disagree. Those people from the other side of the Great Lake did us a favor by dealing a lethal blow to our sworn enemy. Why would we wish to help the Acolhua scum now that they are powerless and squashed? Why would we hurry to expend our efforts against those who have done this? Why would we close ourselves off in our mountains now that our traditional enemy is humbled? What will we offer to our gods if no raids were sent against the Lowlands' settlements?"

Marveling at the composure of her husband, Mino heard him saying, "We will feed our gods with the hearts of the warriors who will try to enter our passes. There will be enough foreigners, the Tepanecs and their allies, who will try to do that. All those will be caught and slain by our brave men, all intruders who try to enter our mountains."

"I think the Honorable Leader is right," said one of the leading warriors. "We should wait and see, watching those invaders, learning their intentions. Until we know better we should not decide on any strategy aside from the one that is making sure our towns and villages are safe."

More voices joined in, murmuring in consent.

"And yet," insisted the thin man, scowling, apparently set on arguing. "May it not be a mistake to not strike our new enemy now, while he is busy subduing the filthy Lowlanders? Before this new enemy has grown too bold, too familiar with our surroundings. With all due respect for our War Leader's claim, we do not know these mysterious Tepanecs well enough to form an opinion."

"*I* know those people well. They will start prowling our mountains, but not before settling their newly conquered lands. We should not provoke them into trying to explore our parts of the land too soon."

Oh, why was he always so fearless, so outspoken at times? wondered Mino, shivering. They all knew of his origins, especially after what had happened three summers ago; yet, why did he remind them of that so openly, so plainly?

"I agree that the strategy of waiting and guarding our passes seems to be the best for the nearest future," said one of the priests quietly.

The voice of Ai rose. "Unless we let them grow too strong and too bold by doing just that."

"They are too strong and too bold already," said the War Leader sharply. "That's how they are, and that's why they are such a dangerous enemy." Mino held her breath, recognizing the slightly strained note to her husband's voice. His patience was wearing off. "They were this way before setting out to cross the Great Lake for the first time, three summers ago, and they were this way long before that."

"Then why should we wait? This dangerous enemy is growing bolder as we speak, accumulating power behind our mountains. Why should we refrain from fighting them?"

"Because they are too strong for us to handle all by ourselves. They are busy plundering the Lowlands now, and we should not provoke them into exploring the Highlands. We should guard our passes until the right time to war on them comes."

"And when might this 'right time' come?"

"When we could join our forces with other nations around the Great Lake." The words of the War Leader rang out clearly, enhanced by the silence that suddenly prevailed.

"Are you proposing to fight the Tepanecs together with the

Acolhua Lowlanders?" asked Ai slowly, as though making sure everyone heard and understood.

Mino winced at the pain as her nails sank into the flesh of her palms.

"Under current circumstances, I believe we may have no choice." Her husband's voice was still calm, but there was a stony ring to it now. She watched him turning toward the frozen members of the council and their guests. "I know these people. I know how their minds work. They are set on conquest, and they will not rest until every *altepetl*, every town, every village around our Great Lake and beyond our valleys are paying them tribute and sending them warriors, to conquer more lands. They have the power and the resources, and they have the determination." He paused. "And yet, they are ruining themselves by extending their conquests. Soon their empire will be too large to handle, and then they'll collapse, pushed over the brink by our Highlander warriors. But to do that, we will need to enlist the support of as many people as we can, from all over our side of the Great Lake. We will have to overcome our differences, our historical enmity for this mutual effort. I wish we could find a better solution, but I do not see any."

The heavy silence seemed to fill the air with something poisonous, difficult to breathe. Even the wind seemed to freeze. Not a leaf rustled, not a branch cracked.

"So this is why we are forced to host the filthy Acolhua, the heir to the Texcoco throne," said Ai slowly, stressing his every word. "That's why mighty *Camaxtli* was refused the opportunity to receive the heart of this highborn Lowlander as an offering?"

Mino held her breath.

"We have a long tradition of taking in refugees," she heard her husband saying calmly, voice just a little too low. *How could he keep so calm at this continued probing against his authority, and before all the respectable people of Huexotzinco?*

"Especially if the War Leader's son is the one to bring the unusual refugee in. An impeccable youth in himself, spending long summers away, fighting alongside gods-know-whom."

The War Leader's voice did not change, but it had a growling tone to it. "The way a refugee, *any refugee,* comes in does not matter. Mighty *Camaxtli* receives worthy offerings. He feeds on the hearts of the captured warriors. Warriors! Not insignificant youths fleeing from their ruined homes. The heir to the Texcoco throne was not an eligible offering. His heart would offend the mighty god, unless captured while fighting against us."

"He would do it, given a chance."

"If he does, then he will no longer be offered shelter here."

More silence. Mino felt the women beside her holding their breath, staring, afraid to miss a word. Even from the distance of their watching place, she could sense the animosity and the suppressed fury. The tempers would fray, she knew, her stomach tightening, turning, her worry overwhelming. *Why, why did he allow Kuini to bring his Lowlander, the heir to the Texcoco throne, here?*

She remembered that autumn, only two seasons ago, when the Tepanecs had invaded again, humbling the Lowlanders successfully and oh-so-very thoroughly this time. Oh, how unsettled, how afraid she had been. She knew how fierce and relentless those Tepanecs were. She knew her husband was doing the right thing by trying to convince their people to help the Lowlanders against all custom and tradition. Only this once. Yet, the council didn't listen.

And then, her son had come back. Just like that, after more than two summers of being away, doing gods-knew-what. Not a boy anymore, but a warrior, tall and broad shouldered, with his head partly shaved and his hair pulled up in the typical topknot of the enemy, his face and his chest sporting new scars, his body brown and well muscled. A man, a seasoned warrior; and yet, still a confused youth, judging by the look in his eyes.

Oh, how relieved she had been, how elated, how glad. Trusting herself to find a way to bridge the gap between him and his father, now that their family was whole again. Yet, her elation had faded upon learning the identity of his companion. Netzahualcoyotl, the First Son of the dead Emperor, the heir to the Texcoco throne. Inconceivable! And completely unacceptable.

She had told her husband all that and more, and yet, the War Leader had refused to do the right thing. Instead, he had argued with his peers, the other leaders, and then the town's council, throwing all his influence, accumulated over so many summers, into convincing them, endangering his status, until the elders of Huexotzinco agreed to give this strange refugee a chance.

Why? she had asked him. *Why?* Their son had no right to demand such a thing, neither from his father, nor from the rest of the town. He had done nothing for his people, and by his age young men were already expected to serve their community. But her husband only grinned mysteriously and told her that the youth might be onto something here, something that could be used for the benefit of their people in the long run.

Tenochtitlan was boiling with discontent, he had told her. And the conquered Acolhua were not happy. By joining forces with those people, the Highlanders might be able to push the Tepanecs back to their side of the Great Lake, and be rid of the dangerous presence once and for all.

However, such an enterprise would take time. It should be planned thoroughly, executed most carefully. And so, as the winter had passed, he had gotten busy prowling around the Lowlands, sending shady delegations of traders to Tenochtitlan to communicate with his brother.

Mino ground her teeth, thinking of her husband's brother. Oh, no, she had never liked this troublesome, dangerous, unpredictable man, his easy charm and confidence notwithstanding. If he dragged her husband into trouble this time, she would make sure to put some curse on him. Something to make him suffer.

Oh, but why, why did this man have to show up after almost thirty summers of separation, and in such a dramatic manner? Why couldn't he just disappear back into oblivion after leaving the Highlands shortly before her son had left? However, since that summer, the brothers had kept in close contact through traders and occasional travelers, and she knew it would not end well. Not for her husband. The war leaders of foreign origins were not supposed to be in touch with any of the Lowlander enemies, the Mexica Aztecs most of all.

"I suppose it is time we break the discussion," she heard the head of the town saying, his words light, not reflecting the certain ring to his voice. It was an order and not a suggestion, and she was grateful for the old man's intervention. It would be better for this particular meeting to be broken.

Watching the elders getting to their feet, stretching their limbs, she became aware of her own cramped muscles.

"Unbelievable," said one of the women, shaking her head. "I thought they would start fighting in front of our eyes."

"Why would they do that?" demanded Mini tersely, trying to conceal her own agitation. "We are not led by youths, but by seasoned, wise people, great warriors and great men."

"The War Leader should not have argued," said another woman. "He is liked and trusted by many, but it all may change in a heartbeat in the current situation. He should not have forced Huexotzinco into taking the Lowlander in."

"He did not force them," exclaimed Mino hotly. "He suggested it, and they saw the force of his argument."

The women smiled knowingly, and she tried to suppress her growing anger.

"Well, this youth is nice and polite, such pleasant company," said a plump woman, the second wife of the previous war leader, now the head of the town. "They would not have tolerated him here otherwise, the War Leader or not." She giggled. "And to think that we host such a highborn Acolhua, the next emperor of the Lowlands, of all things. Unbelievable! Your son must have been a searching youth to pick this sort of an exotic company."

Straightening her shoulders, Mino shrugged. "My son should have known better than to go away into the Lowlands in the first place. I don't like any of this any more than you all do, but my husband is right. We cannot war on these people now, and we will have to join the Lowlanders when they rebel."

"The Lowlanders will never rebel. They are conquered and destroyed. They will never be able to raise their heads again. And it's a good thing, if you ask me." The Chief Wife of the council member shrugged. "Your husband may nurture some strange ideas, Priestess, but he should be careful sounding them aloud."

"My husband knows what he does, and I hope our people will

not hurry to forget everything he has done for Huexotzinco."

Concentrating on their step, the women began to descend the trail leading back to the town, avoiding Mino's challenging gaze. Cowardly rats, she thought. But they were right. He was too careless, too convinced of the rightfulness of his chosen course. Was it the time to make a special offering in her temple? Maybe the goddess would help.

CHAPTER 6

Coyotl stretched luxuriously, watching the afternoon sun painting pretty pictures on the nearby cliff. It was full of dancing shadows, because of the light breeze playing in the treetops, and the glassy surface of the stone glowed at him merrily, reflecting his mood.

The girl's head was heavy on his arm, and her earpiece left a deep print on his skin, still he did not bother to move, unwilling to disturb her. They had been drifting like this, between the pleasant reality and the light sleep since the early afternoon, making love in between the rests.

She turned out to be a wonderful lover. Better than any girl he had lain with before, soft, trim, and delightfully responsive, eager to do many things before he even realized he had wanted to do them.

"It's getting late," she muttered sleepily, not attempting to get up.

"No. No late," he said, running his palms along the smoothness of her stomach. "Don't want you go."

She stretched lazily, and there was a smile on her face as she raised her head. "I have a long way to go yet."

"I take back," he said, pulling her closer. "Take you, your village."

She regarded him thoughtfully as if weighing her possibilities. "No, you can't take me back. People may see us. But I suppose we still have a little time…" The playfulness of her smile made him dizzy.

As she slid alongside him, he helped her eagerly, marveling at the touch of her warm, silky skin. Naked, she was a thousand fold more attractive than in her pretty dress, decorated with pelts. Her arms and legs may not have been as smooth as those of the noblewomen or even some of the slave girls in the Texcoco Palace – hers were weathered and bore witness to the hard work of a village woman – still they had their own magic, and her stomach and thighs were deliciously soft.

"You are insatiable," she growled, making herself comfortable on top of him. "I didn't think Lowlanders were such ardent lovers."

He didn't answer, didn't even try to understand her words, too busy with the wonderful sensation to bother with the still-foreign-sounding tongue. Oh, but he had needed this badly, he realized, watching her sparkling eyes, teasing even now, in the middle of the lovemaking.

Oh, yes, she was a tremendous girl, he decided, moving along with the pulses of her body, helping her to climb to the heights of the delight too, seeing her eyes clouding, losing their defiant superiority. Before letting himself go, he thought that the woods were a wonderful place to make love, much better than the Texcoco Palace that lacked in privacy at times.

The sun was already kissing the tops of the trees on the other side of the river when they began gathering their trampled clothes.

"I will have to wash up on my way back," she said, smoothing her hair with both hands. "I hope I don't look like someone who rolled in the grass through the whole afternoon." She pulled a face, fishing green leaves out of the tangles.

"You look that, you do," he said, watching her attempting to braid her hair. "Say them you fall, fall on your way."

She giggled. "Oh, yes. I fell and rolled all the way down to my village. They are sure to believe that." Shrugging, she went on working on her braids. "Never mind. My man should still be away and others wouldn't care. He has no other wives yet, no one to pay attention."

"I wait tomorrow here. Wait you come," he said, peering at her.

Her eyes sparkled. "Maybe. Maybe I'll come." A veiled glance measured him pointedly. "You really *are* insatiable. All this lovemaking should be enough to make a man happy for half a moon and more. A normal person would be more than satisfied." Her eyebrows arched. "But then, when one is supposed to be the Emperor of the Lowlands, one should be ready for all those wives and concubines, eh? To keep those women happy and satisfied, so they won't look for forbidden pleasures elsewhere." Eyes challenging, she gazed at him. "How many women did your father hold in the Palace?"

He frowned, not liking to think about his beautiful Texcoco. "Many women. Can't count."

"But your mother was the Chief Wife, the Empress?"

"No, she not first, in the beginning. But later, yes."

She glanced at him, surprised. "Not first? How so?"

"There was, was another. But later Emperor put aside, the Chief Wife, make my mother the first."

Forgetting her braid, she peered at him, wide-eyed. "It's all true, eh? The Palace and the Emperor. You truly lived it, didn't you?" Eyes losing their usual cheekiness, she gazed at him, shaking her head. "It feels like a tale of a storyteller. But you lived it all, for real!"

Finding it difficult to follow her rapid speech, he grimaced, then busied himself with his loincloth. "I no emperor, not anymore. It's all," he hesitated, searching for the right word, annoyed with it all, his inability to talk properly and his ruined future. "All no more. So forget!"

She came closer, resting her palm on his chest.

"I know it's all gone." Her voice held none of its usual baiting brazenness. "But you lived it all the same. And it's amazing. Think about it." Her eyes sparkled, filling back up with mischief. "And I got to make love to an almost-emperor. Even if it was in the woods. Tomorrow I'll come, and you'll tell me more about it. Tell me what you would do to me if we were in the Palace. In one of those rooms with many pretty things."

His gloom lifting, he grinned at her, thinking of his set of rooms, or better yet, those of his father, the Emperor. The spaciousness of the plastered walls adorned with carved wood, the glittering statues, the reed podiums, the soft mats covered with embroidered cushions. Oh, he would have made love to her in every corner of the Emperor's quarters and then in the throne hall as well, appalling his servants and subjects.

Grinning, he shook his head. "Yes, I make love to you, every place, every room, on..." For his life he could not remember how they say the word "throne," if they had a word for this thing at all. "On emperor seat and where emperor sleep, and gardens, too." Her sparkling eyes made him search his memory for more places. "Behind golden statue, there niche, and in emperor's baths." The thought of her naked in the steam bath made him stir anew. Oh, he did miss bathing properly. "Make plenty love in the baths."

She pressed against him, clearly aroused as well, hanging on every word, as if he talked as eloquently as the best of orators.

"Oh, yes," she whispered. "We would do all of it and more, and you would make me your Chief Wife. I would make a good Empress, you'd see. I swear I could have managed."

Amused, he watched her, wishing to laugh, wiser than to do that. Had she said it seriously? He thought of his mother, the last empress, and Iztac Ayotl's mother, the Tepanec who had preceded her, an immensely more prominent and dominant woman. Both had been great empresses, different in their behavior, but both oh so well groomed and so well educated, both noblewomen with precious aristocratic blood running through their veins.

He laughed, squeezing her in his embrace. She would make a good concubine though, he decided, not bothering to sound his thoughts aloud. He still wanted her to come here on the next day.

As they made their way down the trail, enjoying the cool breeze of the nearing evening, he pondered how close to her home he should take her. Not to her village surely, that would be too obvious, and anyway, he may not find his way back. They were still around Huexotzinco, in the woods he had come to know well enough, yet her village might be well away from his range of familiar surroundings.

As if listening to his thoughts, she slowed her steps, reaching the end of the trail and the clearer view of the river.

"You wait here tomorrow," she said briskly, back to her commanding self. "Somewhere around the early afternoon. I may be late, so wait patiently. I have chores to do. My man should be back soon, and he won't like his house all neglected and dirty."

He winced at the mention of her man, having forgotten all about it through the wonderful afternoon. "I wait, early afternoon."

With a playful grin, she turned to go, yet the sound of hurried footsteps made them both tense. Someone was coming up the path from the direction of the river, climbing the cliff, hopping from rock to rock lightly, self assuredly.

Gesturing for her to stay where she was, Coyotl neared the edge where he could see the narrow path, twisting between the protruding stones like a thin serpent. The wide shoulders of the climbing figure and the stub of his half-grown hair made him sigh with relief.

"Up here," he called, waving his hand.

Kuini's broad face beamed at him from below. "I've been looking for you all over, you dirty piece of dung," he shouted, doubling his step.

"Who is there?" asked the girl suspiciously, not attempting to come nearer, poised on the top of their previous trail, ready to flee.

"It's just friend. My friend. Oh!" Her darkening face made him remember. "I forget..."

"I'm leaving," she said, not attempting to move. "And if your friend shows up here again, I'm not coming back. Do you understand? I come back tomorrow only if he does not—"

Her speech cut short, she glared at Kuini, who appeared behind the cliff, sweating and short of breath. Coyotl felt like cursing and laughing at the same time. How ridiculous!

"I've been running all over these cliffs since midday." Kuini's eyes twinkled, brushing past the girl, clearly missing her open animosity. "I see you've been busy. A nice pastime."

However, his Nahuatl only served to make her angrier.

"Look who is here," she said icily, voice trembling with disdain. "A wild warrior and a lousy hunter. What honor!"

Kuini stared at her, perplexed. "What?"

"Don't stare at me like you didn't know any of it. You are all of that and more!"

"Who is this fox, and what does she want?" asked Kuini, turning to Coyotl, eyes wide. He didn't switch to Nahuatl this time, so the girl had her chance to turn yet angrier.

"You know very well who I am," she hissed. "And you are not worthy of my time!" Turning abruptly, she ran up the trail, her knee-length skirt swirling angrily, the hastily made braid bouncing.

"What, in the name of the Underworld…"

Coyotl took his gaze off the swaying bushes, then shrugged. "She doesn't like you."

"I can see that, but why?"

"You took her some summers ago, didn't you?"

"What? I don't even know her!"

Watching his friend's stupefied face, Coyotl wanted to laugh, but somewhat bitterly. There went his pleasant afternoon of the next day.

"She says you did. She is still angry with you because of that." He remembered his conversation with her from the previous day. "She said you promised to make her your woman or something."

Kuini's face grew more bewildered. "This *cihua* of yours has great imagination. But I hope she was worthy of your time."

"Oh yes, she was. Many times, too."

"Nice!" Kuini shifted his weight from one foot to another.

"Yes, it's a nice pastime. You should get busy too, instead of sneaking around the passes, wasting your time spying on the Tepanecs."

"Oh yes. Let them come here undisturbed. I really should lay with every *cihua* around the Highlands before they come here and take them all for themselves."

Coyotl winced, sobering. "They won't come up here. They wanted Texcoco and the Acolhua provinces."

"Of course they will. Two days ago, when we went down there on that excursion that you refused to hear about, who do you think was lurking right past one of the passes? Those same

Tepanecs, confident and happy. Five warriors, five hunters."

"They don't have hunters."

"Oh, whatever. Peasants. Traders. Not warriors, anyway."

"Peasants, yes. Or maybe servants."

"Who cares? They were there, entering the Highlands, busy hunting like the place was already theirs."

"Did you fight them?"

"Yes. Killed a few. Not all of them, though. If you were there we would have finished the whole bunch together." Kuini shrugged. "But that was not why I was looking for you. Listen—"

Horrified, Coyotl stared at his friend. "Did you try to trap ten Tepanecs all alone?"

"No, of course not! But those good-for-nothing's who went with me were useless."

"I'll come with you next time, I promise." Guiltily, he watched his friend, taking in the tired features and the fresh cut above the wide forehead, hiding in the half grown hair. "I'm sorry. I should have come. It's just that I hate to see what is happening in my lands, and I don't see any point in going down there to watch it. It's useless. The Tepanecs are now ruling my provinces, and the Aztecs are looting my *altepetl*." He felt his nails sinking into his palms and welcomed the pain. It took the edge off his bottomless desperation.

Kuini's face darkened. "You may have no choice but to come next time." He looked around, then began descending the trail back the way he had come.

"What do you mean?" called out Coyotl, refusing to move.

"Come. We need to talk."

Head reeling, thoughts in turmoil, Coyotl followed, the sensation of a looming disaster gripping his insides. When his friend turned sharply, leaving the path and starting to make his way between the rocks, he asked no questions, suddenly not sure he wanted to know the news.

Up on a small shelf, Kuini stopped, turned around and smiled. "Here we can talk without being overheard." Oblivious to the height, he sat upon the very edge and let his feet dangle free. "Up there it seems pretty secluded and all, but I just found out that when the wind is right, someone hiding behind the trees can hear you well enough."

"How did you find out?" asked Coyotl, forcing himself to sit beside his friend, uncomfortable with the height and the sight of the distant rocks lining the shore. "Who did you try to overhear?"

"No, it's not me. But there was this girl..." Kuini frowned. Brushing his palm against his forehead, he peered into the distance and did not finish his sentence.

The silence prevailed.

"The thing is," he said finally, "I came back to the town this morning and people were all busy talking about the gathering of the leaders from all around Huexotzinco." He paused again, as if pondering on how to proceed.

"Yes, I know," said Coyotl. "I heard that too." He measured his friend with a glance. "Come to think of it, where did you spend the night? You obviously did not come back from this raid this morning."

Kuini shrugged and did not take his gaze off the distant cliffs. "No. I slept outside. Didn't feel like spending time in the town. It's nice outside now that the spring is here."

"Did you sleep in the woods?"

"No, not exactly. There was this place..." The Highlander shook his head resolutely. "The thing is, when I came back and heard about the meeting, I wanted to know what was going on. When they are holding those gatherings outside the council house it's their own fault if people eavesdrop."

"What did you hear?"

"Many things, some quite unpleasant." Kuini's lips tightened. "Some people are unhappy with my father's way of handling the situation. One annoying bastard argued openly, questioning some of his decisions. Your presence here, for one." The strong jaw of the Highlander hardened. "He nearly accused him openly! Would you believe that? My father handled it well. He is such a great man. And many people surely saw the reasonableness of his arguments. Still, I suppose there are those who were thinking he may be wrong, and now they received more food for their thoughts."

Coyotl heard his friend grinding his teeth. "What else didn't they like, aside from his consent to give me shelter?" Listening to the ring of his own voice, so calm and even, he marveled at the fact, as his heart made strange leaps inside his chest, and his limbs went quite numb.

"He was not the one to give you the shelter here. The elders of the town, the heads of the clans, were the ones to agree. He is the War Leader, and he is allowed to advice. That's all." Kuini shrugged. "But, yes, I think he was the one to convince them when we came here before the Cold Moons. Anyway, in the sphere of his influence, where he does make the decisions, is the whole situation in your Lowlands. And he says we should not provoke the Tepanecs by continuing to raid the Lowlands as though nothing happened. He says we should only watch our passes, make sure no Tepanecs are venturing here. Nothing more." He paused, took a deep breath. "He says we should wait, then join our forces with your Acolhua people when they rebel."

Coyotl's heart missed a beat and he turned his head so abruptly, his legs swayed, causing him to nearly lose his balance. Heart pounding, he clung to the warm stones of their shelf with his sweaty palms, his breath coming in gasps.

"No need to kill yourself over this." Kuini grinned, amused for the first time. "Apparently, he thinks it'll happen. Apparently, he even counts on it. But he has to convince many people. Many people who do not share his point of view, and, well, he is a foreigner himself, as you know." Another shrug. "He is a brave man and very forceful, but I'm not sure he can go against the traditional ways this time. Too many people will oppose him and his ideas."

Coyotl swallowed. "What does it mean for me?"

He watched Kuini staring into the deepening dusk. "We may have to leave Huexotzinco."

"Where to?"

"I don't know. I'll think of something. But I'll have to talk to him first." He turned his head and gazed at Coyotl, his eyes flat. "We may need to go before someone decides you should go, or worse. Not because of your safety. He may be able to protect you.

He has a lot of influence. Still, I want us to go before it comes to that. I don't want him to endanger himself, or his position, because of something I might have forced on him." The large eyes narrowed. "I hope you understand that."

"Yes, I do," said Coyotl gruffly. To clear his throat proved a necessity. "I understand. And you don't have to leave because of me. I'll manage." He took a deep breath. "I mean it!"

The eyes peering at him relaxed almost visibly. Then a smile dawned, the familiar amused, mischievous grin. "Oh, I'm not going away because of you. I'm sick of this place. I left here three summers ago, and I never intended to come back. So it has nothing to do with you. Should they decide they would be happy to have you here forever, to make you the Emperor of the Highlands, I would still leave."

His heart beating fast, Coyotl watched his friend turning to look at the river, lips twisted, stretched in a contented smile. The knot in his throat tightened. Unable to take his gaze away, he studied the proud profile and the stub of unruly hair where it was supposed to be shaven.

"You are a great friend," he said quietly. "Better than anyone could ask for. I will never, never forget!"

Embarrassed, he turned away too, watching the river. It twisted far below their feet, glittering like a snake in the deepening dusk.

"You seem to like it here, don't you?" asked Kuini after a while. "All this freedom to roam around, hunting and fooling with girls. I can just imagine you settling with this or that local *cihua*, breeding and bringing home food."

Coyotl laughed, suddenly lighthearted and at peace. "Those local girls are something. This Iso-girl, oh man, she really made me work, you know. She just kept going on and on. A great sport."

Puzzled, he saw his friend straightening up.

"Iso," cried Kuini out. "Oh gods, I think I remember her." His face twisted as if he had eaten an unripe fruit. "She may be right about what she said. I think I lay with her once, a long time ago." His grin widened. "My first time. How could I have forgotten?"

"She is really angry with you, you know?"

"Oh, she should have forgotten too by now. It's silly of her to remember."

"Maybe you were her first as well."

"No. I remember that clearly now." The broad face darkened, then closed. "It's entirely different when it's a girl's first time. I had another girl after that. It was her first time. And… you don't forget anything like that. I wish I could meet her again."

"Who was she? A pretty fox from somewhere around?"

The silence hung for so long, Coyotl assumed his friend had sunk too deeply into his thoughts to hear the question.

"No. She was from the Lowlands." It came out quietly, barely overcoming the rustling of the wind.

"Oh, this or that captive?"

"No, no. Nothing like that." Kuini straightened up, shaking his head as if trying to get rid of the memories. "I guess we should get back, to see what's happening." He glanced at Coyotl. "Be careful, and stay within an easy reach. I'll talk to my father, then I'll let you know. If I can't get to him tonight, then we'll see what's happening tomorrow. Either way, we'll sort it out in the next few dawns."

CHAPTER 7

Dehe crouched above the small row of plants, pulling at occasional weeds that pushed themselves between her precious growths. She loved tending her tiny garden that she had made sure to create as soon as she had found this brook and this cave, deciding to make them her temporary home.

Wiping her forehead, she looked at the sun. It was already late into the afternoon, and she contemplated going down to the river for a good swim. At this part of the day the women would usually be done with their laundry, and the men, coming from the fields or the woods, would be done with their washing as well. She didn't want to face any of them, unwilling to endure their wondering glances. She was fed up with Huexotzinco and its citizens, all of them. Well, maybe not all of them, but with the most.

She shook her head, thinking about last night and that strange Lowlander-looking warrior, the son of the War Leader and the annoying priestess. Did she truly invite him to come here, the place she had arranged for herself since running away from the town? And after he had frightened the life out of her with his sudden appearance and his chasing her in such a wild, brutal way?

It seemed impossible, inappropriate, yet she had done just that. Invited him to wash up in the small brook she had come to regard as her own, then proceeded to examine his wound – a superficial cut above his temple, nothing to worry about – then allowed him to stay for the night in her improvised home, her small cave padded with blankets she had stolen from the last family that had housed her. He didn't ask, but somehow it felt natural that he should stay. He didn't seem too eager to go back to the town as well.

Grinning, she remembered how tense she had grown, how unsettled as the darkness descended. What if he tried to force her into something she wouldn't want to do? He was a warrior, strong and grim, probably willful and spoiled, used to have his way with women. She had been all nerves, but it all came to nothing. Dead tired, he had just fallen asleep shortly after she had finished smearing an ointment on his head. Just like that. No effort to talk, no demand to eat something, no attempt to take advantage of her. One moment awake and deep in his thoughts, the next asleep, curled up on her favorite blanket, hands spread, hair plastered over his sharp cheekbones, eyes closed, peaceful, and not especially imposing, not anymore. She had watched him for a long time, amazed, and maybe even a little disappointed at being safe, after all.

She shook her head at the strange memory, then wiped the sweat off her forehead. Time to wash up. Straightening up, she caught her breath. The voices pounced on her out of nowhere, giving her barely enough time to dive behind the protective darkness of the cliff. Some men seemed to advance along the invisible path, heading deeper into the woods.

"You should not have come out against the War Leader so openly," said one of the voices, proceeding casually along the trail. "It was not wise to do that."

Hands trembling, Dehe clung to the damp rock, her heart thundering in her ears, interrupting her ability to listen. She could hear them halting abruptly, one of the voices vibrating angrily in the deepening dusk.

"That man went too far! He can't force us into following him blindly, doing what he thinks fit all the time."

"He was our War Leader for half of twenty summers," said another one thoughtfully. "He proved himself worthy of following."

"But not blindly, never blindly!" exclaimed the second man. "He seems to forget we are no Lowlanders. We don't have an emperor to lead us and to tell us what to do. We have the heads of the clans to direct us." She could hear the speaker drawing a deep breath. "Yet, since the first Tepanec invasion, this man is trying to force us into doing something that goes against our heritage, our history, our traditions."

"He presents his unusual ideas well." The first man's voice began drawing away. She could hear the branches cracking under the feet of the other two. "He may be correct with his assumptions, far-fetched as they may sound."

"Or he may be incorrect," rasped the angry man hotly, following his peers. "But either way, what makes my nerves prickle is the way he is arguing, too forcefully, too strongly. He has no respect for other people's opinions."

Breathing with relief, Dehe felt her taut nerves calming. They were leaving, those invaders of her private corner of the forest. Carefully, she peeked out in time to see their backs disappearing into the brownish foliage.

So they were unhappy with the War Leader, she thought, amused now that the danger was over. Little did they know! What would they say if she was to tell them about that meeting their glorious leader was having with some foreigner, speaking Nahuatl in the very heart of their mountains?

She chuckled, then glanced at her plants. They needed watering, she reflected, the voices still there, reaching her faintly through the thickening dusk. Undecided, she hesitated. It would be stupid to follow them, stupid and dangerous. Paces light, she slid along the invisible path, disturbing no leaf.

The three men were still there, lingering on the edge of the clearing.

"You don't like his ideas, that's all," the thickset man was saying. She recognized his voice as the one who had spoken in a calm, thoughtful manner. He still sounded that way. "He doesn't force anything on anyone. The War Leader has always been respectful of our ways, even if he was born a foreigner. He has been one of us for too long to think of himself as belonging to any other peoples. He has been entrusted with the task of leading our warriors and planning our raids. He is one of us."

His companion, a slight, slim-looking man, broke a thin branch off of the tree next to him.

"And yet he tries to bring us upon a strange path that goes against our traditions and our way of life." The angry man paused. "He tries to bring us to fight alongside our sworn enemy, for the mighty gods' sake!" The gnarled fingers broke the branch in two, crushing the spiky edges. "I think his foreign blood is now choosing the words coming out of his mouth. And I also think it came to pass in his youngest of sons. This strange youth who has spent long moons amongst our enemies of his own free-will, fighting together with the Lowlanders, imagine that. And here he is, coming back all of a sudden, bringing along the son of the Acolhua Emperor, no more, no less." The branch cracked, breaking into smaller fragments. "So now, we are forced to host our arch-enemy, sheltering him against the wrath of those unknown Tepanecs, the same people our fearless leader is so afraid of." Angrily, the man threw the pieces of bark away. "The youth is unimportant, but without his father he would never be heard or listened to. And Huexotzinco would not be forced into this ridiculous situation."

Another spell of silence prevailed. Dehe pressed against the damp trunk of a tree, afraid to be discovered, afraid to miss a word. They were talking about *him*, that youth who had looked like a Lowlander and who had spent the night in her makeshift home.

"If you want to do something, maybe you should leave the War Leader and concentrate on this young hotheaded son of his," said the third man, resuming his walk. "The youth can be provoked into doing stupid things. He is angry and violent. And then, maybe his father will get in trouble on account of him. Who knows? An incident or two may discredit our fearless leader in the eyes of many people."

This time, she did not hesitate. Afraid to breathe, her limbs numb and acting as if on their own, she followed them soundlessly, all ears.

"It may work," agreed the thin man more calmly, watching his feet as if afraid to step on something. "It may be worth a try. This may keep the man too busy to argue and try to convince everyone to make the Lowlanders rebel. What a ridiculous notion!"

"He may be in no position to argue anymore." The voice of the third man was hardly audible. Even his companions raised their heads in an attempt to listen.

"It won't get that far!" breathed the first man. "He is a good leader, and we should not plot against him."

The cloak of the thin man rustled angrily as he whirled around. "We are not plotting anything. The young hothead and his Acolhua friend have all the chances to get into trouble. It's a wonder they made it peacefully so far. And if it affects the War Leader, then it's too bad. But it's his son, and it's his problem that the young beast is so wild. It's certainly not our fault." The man glanced at his companions, then turned around and resumed his walk. "He is growing old. Maybe it's time someone younger took his position."

"No, the man is a good leader, and he should lead our warriors for more summers to come," stated the first man sharply. "I will not agree to replace him just because some of you are not entirely happy with his proposed solutions to all sorts of situations."

For a while nothing but the sound of their paces interrupted the silence. Pleased with her soundless steps, Dehe followed, surer of herself. She was a part of these woods, they were not. They were the invaders, going about, plotting against the War Leader, trying to get at the man through him, the wild youth who had fallen asleep not trying to take any advantage of her.

She recalled watching him sleeping, lit by the spare moon, his strong, sharp-angled face bruised, sporting a scar and a little facial hair, a man, a dangerous warrior, yet also a boy, seeming in his sleep to be calm and somehow unprotected. She had watched him for a long time, fighting the urge to touch his cheek, to find out what it'd feel like against her palm.

"We are not plotting anything against anyone," she heard the slim man saying. "I'm just sounding my opinions which I was not allowed to sound in the meeting!"

Dehe stifled a gasp as a small rabbit leaped from under her feet, its brownish fur blending perfectly against the muddy ground. Heart thumping, she held her breath as the men on the clearing fell silent.

"What was that?" asked the slim man, straightening his shoulders. Eyes narrowing, his gaze brushed past the trail and the thick trees, and Dehe froze, fighting the rising wave of panic. He could not see her the way she was half crouched behind the thick tree, still, his eyes scanned her direction, and her senses screamed danger.

The rabbit darted back into the woods, and the other two men laughed.

"You are not at your best today, Ai," commented one of them.

The slim man shook his head curtly. "No, something is wrong," he said, seeming to peer right at Dehe.

He hesitated, then, moving with a surprising agility for a man of his age, he leaped back toward the trail, halting among the thick trees, listening attentively. So close she could smell the faint odor of sweat and hot beans surrounding him, Dehe froze, her heart coming to a halt. One heartbeat, then another. Pressing against the rough bark, she held her breath, ordering her senses not to panic the way she had panicked on the day before. There was no chance of him discovering her.

"Come, brother," called one of the others. "There is no one here."

She could hear the man turning slowly, then hesitating again. Suddenly, the rustling of his steps neared. With the remnants of her self control, not daring to breathe at all, she took a careful step, then another. All she had to do was to dive into the safety of the woods. Why had she followed these men in the first place?

He was beside her before she understood what had happened, grabbing her arm in a painful grip, making her whirl around. But for the rough fingers digging into her shoulder, she would have lost her balance.

His haggard, sweaty face swept before her eyes, but she didn't waste her time on studying it. Using the drive her body had gained while being turned so forcefully, she let it continue its fall, throwing herself on, feeling the fingers that were digging into her skin slipping, fighting for a grip. Stifling a cry, she wriggled from the other hand that tried to grab her, then literally rolled away.

Wild with panic, she scrambled to her feet, charging straight through the bushes, running pell-mell, oblivious of the brunches flogging her limbs. She could hear their cries and the sound of their feet, but it drew away quickly. Still, she didn't dare to stop until reaching the cliffs facing the river. There she slowed a little, to catch her breath and to find a good trail to descend safely, not daring to look back or to think about what had happened. Did this man know who she was?

Careful not to slip on the damp rocks, she headed down the trail. What would important people know about the insignificant, foreign girl? Still, they would wish to find her now, knowing that what she had overheard was important. She shuddered. *Oh gods, what now?*

The darkness was descending. She could see the first stars glimmering in the graying sky. To go back to her makeshift home? But they might be combing the woods now.

The river was near, and she paused, pitting her face against its refreshing breeze. She should sleep somewhere down there and then go away in the morning, just like she had intended to do in the first place. Maybe it was all for the best.

Up on the river bank, she hesitated once again. The occasional lights of the town, just beyond the bend, beckoned. Maybe she would do better going there and finding this youth. He should be there now, somewhere in Huexotzinco. She could tell him what she had heard and maybe he could help her to organize her journey. She would need to take things along, food and blankets, and some spare clothes.

Resolutely, she turned around and headed toward the lights.

Mino watched her husband pacing the wooden tiles of the floor, back and forth, back and forth, like a caged jaguar, his steps wide and springy, catlike as always.

Despite her mounting worry, she smiled, remembering that it

was the first thing she had noticed about him while seeing him for the first time, oh some many summers ago. Another lifetime. Many lifetimes.

Had she truly been a slave smuggled out of Tenochtitlan by his brother and the Tepanec warrior who had fallen in love with her? It all seemed like a blurry forgotten dream. On the rare occasions she cared to remember, she would wonder if maybe she had dreamed it all up, in reality never having left her mountains. But then, if that were so, how had she come to share her life with this outlandish man, the man whose speech was still accented, whose ways were independent, and whose thinking was special, strikingly irregular.

She didn't try to hide her grin, remembering seeing him for the first time, a youth training with his brother and his friends, all of them imposingly tall Tepanecs, all but him. Yet, he was as good, better than many, making up for his lack of height and broadness with this same catlike swiftness and fierceness. Still looking outlandish, even among his own people.

"How dare he, this dirty descendant of a rat!" he exclaimed once again, bringing her back from her wandering through the mists of the past. "To question my decisions so openly and in front of the clan elders, of all things! I swear I have never found it more difficult not to kill someone." He smashed his fist against the wooden pole of the doorway. "And the filthy piece of excrement just went on and on, spilling it all. First, doubting my strategy against the Tepanecs; then, bringing up the Acolhua heir. He even had the gall to hint about the doubtful actions of my son, imagine that! The only thing he neglected was to bring up my foreign origins." Another offensive shook the hapless pole. "I'm telling you, this filthy piece of dirt is up to something."

"He didn't have to bring up your origins, because you bothered to do it yourself," said Mino mildly, pursing her lips.

He whirled at her. "I have never tried to conceal my origins. It is there for everyone to see and ask questions, if they feel curious. I never tried to pass for an impeccable Highlander. There is nothing new about that."

"I know, I know," she said hurriedly, filled with compassion.

He was such a proud man. "But you did bring it up in the wrong way this time. You let them feel ignorant on the subject that is preying on everyone's mind. You threw it into their faces. You let them feel like you know better. It made them feel bad about themselves. And that is exactly what pushes some people into turning obtuse and aggressive."

He studied her, his eyes dark and flashing.

"You may be right." Then he shrugged and resumed his pacing. "Still, I know I am right about that. I know the Tepanecs better than our people think, better than most of the Lowlanders even. They can lose a battle, but they cannot be stopped. What happened in the Lowlands should have taught us a lesson. The Acolhua won many battles. The first Tepanec invasion was repulsed, their side of the Great Lake had been invaded, and still they refused to make peace. They just regrouped and resumed their offensive as if the two summers of their defeats had never happened. And now, here they are, ruling the Lowlands, getting organized below our mountain passes." He peered at her fiercely. "Our people have trusted me for summers. Why would they stop trusting me now?"

She took a deep breath. "I think you made a mistake when you allowed Kuini to bring the Acolhua heir here."

That made him stop once again. Frowning, he studied the low table in front of him.

"I may be wrong, but I think our son saw something we missed." Grinning mirthlessly, he shook his head. "This boy has more to him than he cares to display. We overlooked him, we always did. He was just that little thing, the last of our children. But three summers ago he showed us his true nature. Only a glimpse of it, yet we kept misunderstanding him. All we saw was the angry, unreasonable youth. But in some way, he showed us that we can get along with the Lowlanders. He lived with them for two summers and now his friend, the heir to the Texcoco throne no more and no less, is living with us, doing better than anyone could have expected."

Are you certain you are not trying to make it up to him? she thought, deciding not to say it aloud.

He looked at her, questioning. "You think I'm wrong in suggesting we help the Lowlanders, don't you?"

"I don't know," she said tiredly. "A part of me screams that the Lowlanders are our avowed enemies and we should never, never, help them out. Yet, another part of me urges me to trust your leadership, as always. You must be right about the Tepanecs. Maybe it's time to overcome our differences and help the Acolhua lowlifes, as much as I detest the very idea of it. For the sake of our independence. Only for this!"

"I never thought to do it for any other reason." His mouth tightening, he watched her through his narrowed eyes. "Or do you also suspect me of hidden motives or affections now?"

She glared back at him. "I never doubted your motives or your intentions, but your opinions, while usually wise, can be influenced, like those of any other person. You keep close contact with your brother since you came to meet him three summers ago. I know you value his word. But he may be pushing you into a wrong direction." She stood the fury of his glare. "I know he is a good man, and I know he has your best interests in his heart, still, he is the warlord of another of our enemy nations. He cannot see the welfare of our people while planning his grand scale schemes."

"Do you think the War Leader of your nation is a man that has no mind of his own?" he asked, voice almost growling.

"No, but I think he can be influenced like any other person."

Muffled voices interrupted the heavy silence, and she turned to the doorway in time to see the massive shoulders of Nihi, her firstborn, preceded by two of the most prominent warriors and the priest of *Camaxtli*, a lean, elderly man of many summers.

"Greetings, Honorable Leader."

She watched her husband's shoulders straightening with an effort as he took a deep breath, striving to appear calm. Her heart twisted. He was a great man, and his courage knew no bounds.

The greetings flowing past her ears, she watched the men arranging themselves upon the mats, unhurried and seemingly at ease, but she could feel their tension lurking near the surface. They all sensed the trouble looming, and they were all her husband's friends.

"So what is it all about, brother?" inquired the priest, as she came back carrying a tray with cups and a flask of *pulque*. "Rumors are plaguing our town, inundating its alleys and pathways. People are frowning and murmuring, anxious, confused."

"The meeting of the leaders was not a peaceful one," she heard her husband saying, calm and in control once again.

"I gathered that much," muttered the priest, his speech difficult to understand even when the man talked loudly due to his mutilated tongue, a result of many summers of daily offerings of his own flesh.

"I hear there is another meeting to be held soon," said one of the warriors, accepting his *pulque* with a polite nod.

"Yes. The Clans Leaders decided to proceed with the discussions on the day after the morrow." The War Leader filled his cup. "Well, I suppose you want to hear what transpired?" he added, tactless as always. "What I have done to make everyone angry."

The eyes of the warriors glittered, and even the priest's lips quivered in amusement. "Yes, brother. Tell us what made everyone so indignant."

"I told them we'll have to help the Lowlanders to rebel against the Tepanecs."

The priest shook his head. "Worse than I thought," he muttered.

"Why would you say something like that?" cried out one of the warriors.

"Because I believe this is the only way to throw the Tepanecs back to their side of the Great Lake. Because we cannot do it alone, and if it is not done they will come to our mountains, and they will take our settlements, despite our attempts to prevent that."

"It will not happen, Father!" cried out Nihi, losing his usual presence of mind. "The Lowlanders tried to do this for countless summers, and they got nowhere. The Tepanecs would take an occasional village, but they would burn it, take the people and go away. They could not stay however much they may wish to do that."

"And this is precisely what I'm trying to tell everyone!" The War Leader's fist crashed against the planks of the low table. "The Tepanecs are no Acolhua Lowlanders. They are thousand fold more powerful, more ferocious, more determined. They are as fierce as we are, but they have all the resources of the Great Empire to rely upon and hordes of warriors from all over the conquered lands. They have taken all *altepetls* up to the western mountains and up to our lands. We are the next target. Do not mistake their idleness of the past seasons. They took their time to explore their newly gained possessions, and they may take a few more seasons before they act. But act they will."

He leaned forward, encircling them with one of his piercing gazes, domineering, making them listen. Mino's heart swelled with pride. He might be mistaken this time, but he was a born leader, reaching his current position against the odds of his wrong origins. She held her breath, waiting for him to continue.

"We cannot hold on against such an enemy, not for long. What happened to the Lowlanders will happen to us, unless we act wisely. And we don't have many choices. We need allies, we need partners, and regretfully, we can't be picky about it. We will have to unite with our historical foe in order to stand against this common enemy." He paused, and she saw his jaw hardening. "And we may even need to seek more allies among other of the Great Lake's nations."

The silence was so heavy she could hear the rustling of the trees, although the wooden screen was closed for a change. The night insects buzzed around the torch fastened into the wall, and the light flickered, casting strange shadows upon the cracks of the floor.

"Which one of the other nations?" asked the second warrior quietly.

Mino saw her husband's eyes turning guarded as he shrugged. "There are many discontent peoples scattered along the Tepanec Empire."

The priest's face grew softer as the sadness flowed through the man's lean features. "Do you communicate with that brother of yours?" he asked softly.

The War Leader's jaw tightened. "Of course, I communicate with my brother," he said, his voice ringing stonily, having a cutting edge to it.

The priest shook his head. "It'll bring no good," he muttered, his gaze leaving his host's face, brushing past the table and the flask of *pulque*, staring blankly ahead.

The cup made a hollow sound banging against the rough planks of the table. "My brother has nothing to do with it."

More silence.

"So you didn't mean to suggest the Mexica Aztecs as our additional allies?" asked the priest as softly as before.

Mino held her breath.

"The Aztecs have allied themselves with the Tepanecs," she heard her husband saying, his voice calm again, even if a little too low. "Those Mexica people are prospering, enjoying the fruits of their relationship with the mighty Tepanecs. I wouldn't expect them to rebel in the near future." He straightened his gaze, let it rest upon his guest's face, his eyes friendly but firm, having some chill in them. "I understand your misgivings. My brother used to be the War Leader of our enemy nation. He is still an influential man, respected and appreciated in Tenochtitlan." The cold gaze did not waver. "Yet, you do not need to doubt my loyalty and the credibility of my judgment because of my family connections. I admit that I would love to see the Aztecs joining our struggle against the Tepanecs. They are fierce, well-organized and their *altepetl* can contribute to our success. However, I do not see it happening. Therefore I will not propose to ally ourselves with the Aztecs. But I do propose to use the plight of the Acolhua Lowlanders for the benefit of our people."

The silence fell. Watching the shadows dancing upon the wall, Mino sat quietly, feeling spent as if after a long, strenuous run. Oh, he talked well. Like always, just like through this day's council meeting, he made perfect sense. And yet...

She took a deep breath, stole a glance toward the priest's face, trying to read the dispassionate features, to see what the clouded eyes held. This man had a great influence in Huexotzinco and the surrounding villages. He was a good man and a friend. But would he back the War Leader up on this?

The priest sighed. "I know your motives are pure, Old Friend. I can see you are sincere in your intentions, and the only thing that concerns you is the well-being of our people." A sad smile lit his face. "I'll think about it, and if I'm still convinced, without your persuasive presence beside me, I'll try to help, try to make people listen."

There were rapid footsteps and the screen covering the doorway screeched. Startled, she turned her head in time to see her youngest son charging in, then halting in an abrupt manner. Freezing next to the poles of the entrance, the youth blinked as the squatting men turned their heads, gazing at him, not especially kind.

"Oh, I apologize," he said, shifting as if about to run back into the night.

The War Leader shook his head as though waking from a dream, staring at his son, visibly trying to concentrate.

"No need to apologize," he said slowly, but Kuini was already halfway behind the doorway.

"I'm sorry. I'll come back later," he muttered, disappearing into the night.

Without thinking, Mino sprang to her feet, feeling as if in a dream herself. A fleeting glance let her know that his guests were still immersed in their private thoughts, watching her husband and the priest. Attracting no attention, she slipped out of the doorway.

"Wait!"

Her son's broad shoulders were still visible beyond the patio, her call causing him to halt reluctantly.

"Are you well?" she asked, reaching him, startled as always by his imposing height and the broadness of his shoulders. How did he turn into such an impressive warrior? When he had left he was just a youth, tall and slender. And full of rage. Well, some things didn't change.

"Yes." He shrugged. "I just wanted to talk to Father."

"Oh, this is an unusual pleasure," she said, then wanted to bite off her tongue. It was not the time to get saucy.

His eyes narrowed. "It's nothing of importance."

"Listen, I think you should talk to him, and, well, don't go away. Stay until his guests leave."

"I'll come back later. Or maybe tomorrow. It's not that urgent."

The familiar frustration with him welled. "You won't come back. Of course, you won't. You don't want to face your problems. You prefer to run away from them."

She saw his jaw tightening. He looked nothing like his father, but the similarities of their body language were there, impossible to miss. "I didn't ask for your advice, Mother."

"No. You didn't. You do whatever you please, but you remember to come here when you need help."

"This is between me and Father."

She clenched her palms to stop them from trembling, the intensity of her rage sudden and unexpected.

"Oh yes, this is between you and him. But I have to watch it, you know. I have to watch you *using* him. I have to watch you making him pay for crimes he did not commit, as if you discovered him hiding something disreputable that he has done. You treat him in the most shameful manner, but you are not beyond expecting him to help you with your most unusual requests. Even if it makes him endanger his position, his life maybe." She took a deep breath, trying to calm herself, knowing she was acting stupidly, attacking him in this way. "You should stay and talk to him," she finished, peering into the darkness of his eyes.

He watched her for a long moment. "I'll come back later," he repeated firmly, lips clasped into a thin line. His wide steps made no sound as his silhouette disappeared down the road.

Trembling, she stood there, oblivious of the wind, her heart beating madly, stomach empty. What was wrong with her, she asked herself helplessly. How much foolishness for one evening? First, arguing with her husband, making him feel bad after a rotten day; then admonishing her son in this way, and just when the youth came to talk to his Father at last, and of his own accord.

She clenched her fists tight. Stupid! Stupid and unworthy of a woman of her status. May these power-hungry Tepanecs and the filthy Acolhua losers, the cause of it all, go into the Underworld, traveling the worst parts of it for more than four cycles of seasons.

CHAPTER 8

Kuini made his way along the dusty road, not sure as to his destination. For a while, he stared at his feet, kicking small rocks, watching them rolling away, his anger difficult to cope with.

So that's what they all thought, he fumed. That he cared for no one but himself, yet was not above asking for help when pressed. He ground his teeth. Well, it was true enough, when he thought about it. He had left, intending never to come back, but back he came, crawling, counting on the help of his powerful father.

He kicked another stone and watched it flying away, hitting the wall of a low building. Oh, what did his mother know about any of it? She paid little attention to anything aside from her goddess and her priestly duties, Huexotzinco, and Father. She knew nothing about the rest of the world, and she couldn't care less. Yet, she presumed to judge him, Kuini; she who had never come down her mountains. What did she understand about the seriousness of the situation? But Father did. The man understood the danger too well, either due to being a Tepanec or because he was a wise, farsighted man. Or maybe because of both those reasons combined.

Shrugging, he lifted his face to the gust of wind. Oh yes, he would have to come back and talk to Father, the sooner the better.

Many people were still outside, walking by or sitting on their patios, cracking nuts. He passed them by, ignoring their glances. Since his return, people were always staring at him, wondering, whispering. He didn't care, understanding their reasons. Yet, sometimes it got on his nerves.

The moon shone brightly, and he could see as clearly as if it were still dusk. But then, it was far from being midnight yet. Reluctant to go to his brother's home, where Coyotl had gone to sleep, he wandered off, enjoying the cool night air.

The Lowlander must have had an exhausting afternoon, he thought, grinning, his anger cooling gradually. Too much lovemaking activity and that Iso-girl must have been truly good.

He tried to remember what it had been like to lay with her, but the memory would not come. Instead, his vision was again filled with the moonlit pond of the Texcoco Palace's gardens and the naked goddess, the Goddess of the Moon, golden and not silvery as he had imagined before.

Aware of the cavity growing under his chest, he pushed those memories away, by now used to shutting them in the far corner of his mind. Instead, he listened to the outburst of laughter coming from behind the low building of the town council, the place where the heads of the clans would usually meet to talk politics or just pass the time of the day. Now, at night, it was deserted, yet a group of youths seemed to congregate around its far corner.

Indifferently, he watched a bunch of girls forming a half circle, facing a small figure pressed against the wall. There was something familiar about the slim silhouette, and he drifted closer, glad to take his attention off his unhappy thoughts.

"So, little witch, tell us again, why did you come here tonight?" demanded an imposingly tall girl. She wore a long dress, and the decorations of her girdle sparkled in the moonlight, tied around her waist, setting off the curves of her voluptuous figure most temptingly. "Amuse us some more."

"I don't have to tell you anything," called the girl, still pressing against the wall. "Leave me alone!"

Recognizing the husky voice, surprisingly low for such a small person, Kuini halted, peering more closely.

"Oh, you will tell us whatever I like, and I will be the one to decide whether to leave you alone or not." The tall girl took a step forward, towering above the smaller one. "Now ask us again how you can find that pretty fellow of yours."

Glaring at her assailant, the forest girl said nothing, while the rest of the group laughed and cheered, and the youths drew closer, expecting more entertainment.

"Come, little witch. Have you lost your tongue?"

"Leave me alone, you stupid, fat lump of meat," cried out the forest girl angrily, surprisingly not afraid. Bringing both arms up with a sudden movement, she pushed her assailant hard, moving with her whole body, obviously putting all her strength into this concentrated attack.

The larger girl, caught by surprise, swayed and almost lost her balance, amidst a wild laughter from the boys.

"You dirty forest rat!" she yelled, as her prey tried to make it past her as fast as she could.

If not for the rest of the girls, she might have made it, reflected Kuini. Yet, with the others blocking her way the forest girl had had no chance.

Her fingers claws, the enraged representative of the local group caught the rim of the smaller girl's gown, pulling so hard that it made her victim whirl around and sway. But despite her unimpressive size, the little witch turned out to be a worthy opponent. Her hands went for the hair of her assailant, pulling it with the same viciousness, making her attacker cry out.

A few kicks were exchanged, and the cheers of the boys grew with both opponents' hands locked safely in the hair of each other. The rest of the girls tried to cheer too, but did so carefully, watching the fight like a pack of hungry coyotes, waiting for a perfect moment to join the struggle.

Pulling and kicking, both girls seemed to be putting all their effort into harming one another. Then, as the taller girl seemed to lose some of her fighting spirit, another girl pushed, her palm smashing against the back of their victim, grabbing her gown, almost tearing the worn leather. The forest girl whirled at her new attacker, but lost her balance and fell onto the muddy ground.

With the rest of the pack joining the fight, kicking heartily at the fallen enemy, Kuini had had enough.

"Stop it, you stupid lumps of dirt," he called, pushing his way through the melee.

The girls gaped at him, while the youths' eyes clouded. He shoved his way past them.

"Get up," he said to the girl, but she didn't wait for his invitation, scrambling to her feet with an impressive speed, seemingly ready to fight off any additional attack.

"Cool it off, wild boy." A wide-shouldered youth parted from the group, stepping forward. Now Kuini recognized some of the faces, seeing Koo and another boy from his ambushing party eyeing him warily, undecided. "Careful not to harm yourself, spilling orders like you were a chief warrior or something," went on the first youth, coming closer.

Kuini measured his opponent with a quick glance, taking in the wide frame and the long knife attached to the youth's girdle.

"Go away." He motioned at the girl curtly, but she didn't move, staring at him, wide-eyed.

"So, our would-be-lowlander has a soft spot for the Tlaxcallan witch." The youth with the knife chuckled. "How touching."

A few laughs came from the girls, but the rest of the youths remained silent, gloomy and tense.

Kuini narrowed his eyes. "Go away," he said pointedly, not overly opposed to picking a fight. It could be a good thing to vent his frustration this way, and it would be especially satisfying with such an arrogant excrement-eater, one who clearly thought the world of himself.

"You go away." The young man's eyes flashed. "Go away, go back to your stupid Lowlander. Or better take him with you and go back where you both came from, back to the filthy losers that are his people."

"Shut up before you get hurt," said Kuini, shrugging. He struggled to keep his face calm, but his palm sneaked to his own girdle as if of its own accord.

Eyes on the reddening face of his rival, his instincts honed, he whirled at the sudden movement by his side, but it was only the girl. Bruised and disheveled, she peered at him from below, eyes imploring.

"Please, let's just go," she said quietly, making a movement as if about to pull at his hand. "You shouldn't pick a fight. Please!"

He stared at her, trying to understand. What she said made no sense.

A growing laughter made him turn back. "Yes, listen to the little witch, wild boy," said his rival. "Go away before you get hurt." Suddenly, the youth's palm shot forward, grabbing the girl's arm. "But leave your girl here. She'll have a better time with us."

Terror filled the forest girl's eyes all of a sudden, the same wild mindless terror he had seen in her face on the day before, while chasing her through the woods. It didn't make sense either, as she seemed angry and not afraid in the least when attacked by her fellow females earlier.

He didn't dwell on these thoughts. His instincts deciding for him, he didn't pause to grab his knife, but hurled himself at his rival instead, his fist crushing into the softness of the youth's belly, his body using the drive to push his gasping rival off his feet. Barely keeping his own balance, he kicked viciously, then spent a heartbeat on pulling his knife out, ready to ward off another attack, glancing at the others who stood there blinking, not yet fully understanding what happened.

The youth on the ground jumped onto his feet with an admirable swiftness, his knife out and ready as well. For a heartbeat they faced each other, breathing heavily.

"You are done for, wild boy!"

"Why bother to get up?" Kuini allowed himself a derisive smile, enjoying his rival's humiliation. "You should have stayed down."

Ducking a thrust of a knife, he sliced at the youth's momentarily exposed side, but his rival was quick, avoiding the cutting touch of the razor-sharp obsidian by arching his body in a precarious manner. Flopping his arms in the air, he wavered, and Kuini pounced to catch him still off balance, only to bump into the girl who was still there, not having the sense to retreat toward the circle of watching youths.

"Go away," he growled, not spending his time on looking at her.

"No, please. You should not, should not fight him."

Her words barely reached him, as he ducked another onslaught of his rival, who, thanks to the stupid girl, had had enough time to recover. This time the knife made a neat slice in Kuini's cloak, brushing against his skin, though not cutting it.

Grinding his teeth, Kuini faked an attack toward his opponent's right shoulder, going for the belly thrust instead. If the youth wasn't quick, he would be done for, yet his body arched once again, twisting as if in a dance, with only the tip of Kuini's knife sliding against his skin, cutting it, but only slightly.

Breathing heavily, they stared at each other with a measure of mutual appreciation. Lips pursed, eyes narrow, the young man attacked anew, this time more carefully. His knife swished by Kuini's cheek, then slid downward, pouncing toward his ribs. A complicated blow that Kuini had difficulty avoiding, hindered by the sword that was attached to his girdle permanently these days. He stumbled and fought for balance, then sensed more than saw his rival leaping to his side.

His senses panicked, and abandoning the struggle for upright position, he threw himself onto the man, heedless of anything besides the location of the pointed dagger. Surprised, his opponent wavered, and together they crashed onto the dusty ground, amidst the gasps of the onlookers.

His hand with the knife caught under the youth's considerable weight, Kuini tried to get hold of his rival's throat, pressing with all his might, knowing he needed to gain supremacy as fast as he could. While standing, a part of his mind was on the young man's friends, ready to fight their possible attack, but now, sprawling on the ground, he would be quite helpless should they decide to join in.

A vicious kick helped him achieve his goal, if only partially, making his rival groan and roll back. With his both hands free, it was easy to leap on top of his prey, yet now, the youth's other hand locked around Kuini's own throat, and he got less and less air.

Near panic again, he concentrated his remaining strength on the drive of his clenched fist, smashing it into the handsome features until the pressure on his throat lessened. Still, his fist crashed into the bloody face several more times before his instincts made him pause.

The stunned silence prevailed, but he still didn't dare to look up. Concentrated on his rival, he lifted his knife, calculating his next move, knowing that now even this youth's friends would not dare to interfere. No one would attempt to stop the end of such hand-to-hand. The frozen eyes of his defeated opponent confirmed that, staring at him, wide-open, wild, and as if mesmerized.

Amidst the deafening silence, like a priest with a sacrificial dagger, he brought the knife up slowly and beautifully, but suddenly it shook and then he was struggling against something that was hindering its progress. Puzzled, he chanced a quick side-glance, his incredulous gaze taking in the forest girl, who had now crouched by his side, hanging onto his arm with both hands.

"Please," she pleaded, eyes frightened and huge, dominating her heart-shaped face completely now. "You must not do this. Please!"

Incredulously, he stared at her, then tried to shake her off, but she clung to his hand with what seemed to be her entire weight, making it impossible to be rid of her unless he took the chance of freeing his defeated enemy in order to hit her.

His mind numb, heart pumping insanely, he tried to understand it all, seeing the bloody face of his rival turning to stare at her too, just as bewildered.

"Get off me," he groaned finally, trying to shake her off once again.

Her face moved closer, came into his full view, pale, agitated but unafraid now.

"Listen to me," she said firmly. "If you kill him, you are in trouble. And your father, too. They want you to kill someone. They need you to do this to get to your father."

He stared into her eyes that now were very close, glowing eerily, huge and very dark. Blinking, he tried to slam his mind into working. What she said did not make any sense, still, somehow he knew she was right.

He shook her hands off his arm, then got to his feet, feeling empty and spent, not sparing a glance for the man on the ground. His eyes encircled the rest of them, bouncing over their puzzled faces. Clearly, they didn't understand any better than he did what had just happened.

Amidst the same heavy silence he readjusted his cloak, then turned to go, knowing that no one would try to deter him or to attack from behind. Still, the sound of hurried footsteps reached him as he went up the road, his heart racing, mind numb and empty of thoughts.

"Wait!" She was beside him, almost running, trying to keep up with his wide steps. "Where are you going?"

He shut his eyes for a heartbeat, attempting to organize his thoughts. *What did she want from him?*

"Please wait."

He slowed his pace. "What do you want?"

Her face fell, losing some of its previous liveliness, making him regret the question.

"I... I came looking for you, because I needed to tell you something," she said after a small pause.

"You came looking for me? Why?"

"I told you, I needed to tell you something."

"What?"

"Well..." She hesitated once again. "Can we stop somewhere to talk?"

He looked around, only now recognizing the outskirts of the town.

"I suppose we can talk somewhere," he said with an effort, still trying to make his mind work. The fragments of what had happened kept surfacing, disturbing in its vividness. He had just come to talk to his father, and here he was, walking away from the youth he had humiliated dreadfully by not killing him after a beautiful hand-to-hand, yet, somehow it related back to his father and this strange girl beside him wanted something from him.

"How about that grove down by the river?" she asked, pointing at the end of the trail.

"Why not?"

They made their way in silence, and he felt his taut nerves calming, his tensed muscles relaxing, the fresh breeze cooling his burning face. She led the way now, again sure of herself, like back in the woods on the previous night.

"Here," she said, climbing the low cliff, her shins muscular and well-shaped, shining gold in the generous moon. "We can talk here."

He watched her as she made herself comfortable upon the edge.

"Aren't you going to sit?"

He squatted beside her, the sight of the dark flow beneath their feet calming.

"I'm sorry about what happened. It's my fault. It happened because of me." She shifted uneasily. "I came looking for you, but when I stopped to ask them, well, they began to laugh and... and then it got out of hand."

"You asked them how to find me?" he repeated, puzzled.

"Well, yes. How could I know where you live?"

"Why were you looking for me?"

She clasped her palms tight. "I overheard people, people from the council, talking about your father."

The fog in his mind seemed to clear all at once. "What did they say?" he demanded, turning abruptly.

She glanced at him, her eyebrows creating a straight line above her troubled eyes. "There were three of them, and they were not happy about the things he said at some gathering."

He felt his muscles tightening again. "What did they look like?"

"Well..." She frowned, wrinkling her nose and suddenly looking even younger than before. Just a child, really. "There was this scary man, old, and thin, and wrinkled. He was the angriest of them all."

"Oh, that's Ai, the same excrement-eater who talked against my father this afternoon." Kuini ground his teeth. "I don't want to know what he says about my father in private!"

He could feel the girl nodding. "Yes, nothing pleasant. He said the War Leader is too forceful and too aggressive, trying to impose his opinions on the others."

"Stinking, dirty, disgusting pieces of rotten meat!" cried out Kuini, clenching his fists. "I can't believe it! He led them for summers, and now he is at fault, because he is able to see further than all of them put together? Ungrateful bastards!"

She peered at him, her face silvery and curiously appealing in the moonlight. "What do you mean? What does he see?"

"He knows we can't fight the Tepanecs alone when they start coming here."

"Who does he want to fight with?"

"The Lowlanders, who else?"

She gasped and turned to him too abruptly, chancing a fall off the cliff. "The Lowlanders? Never!"

"Why not?"

"They are the dirtiest lowlifes in the whole world. The cruelest, the meanest, the most hateful creatures in the whole world of the Fifth Sun!"

He could hear her breath coming in gasps. Shrugging, he watched the blackish mass of water sparkling below their feet.

"I lived with them for two summers. My best friend is an Acolhua Lowlander. They are people like anybody else."

"No, they are not!" Her voice shook, and he could hear her drawing a deep, convulsive breath.

A glance at her silhouetted figure confirmed what he expected to see – the set lips, the tight jaw, the protectively hunched shoulders, the clenched fists.

"Where are you from?" he asked.

It took her a long time to respond, and he thought she would not answer him at all.

"The other side of the Tlaxcala Valley. Two days walk from their second main town."

"Your village was taken by the Lowlanders." He made it a statement.

She said nothing, but her shoulders hunched as if she was trying to fold into herself.

"Listen," he said. "Those things happen. It happens everywhere. The Lowlanders' towns and their *altepetl* were taken too, by the Tepanecs. But before that, we took one Tepanec town as well. Burned some of their villages too." He shrugged. "It's nothing. It happens everywhere. You were lucky to survive and not to be captured. You should forget it and start living your life anew."

She didn't move, didn't make a sign that she had heard him at all. She just sat there like a stone statue, with only fringes of her disheveled hair fluttering in the wind.

"They came before the dawn, and they burned our homes. I woke up and it was all smoke and screaming. People were running and crying and howling, and things were falling all around us. Wherever we ran there was a fire, and the warriors. They were cutting people. Chopping off their limbs as if they were hunted deer. Opening their stomachs like you open a gourd. It smelled so bad. And the people were twisting and shrieking, or making funny sounds." Her voice rang monotonously, lacking in emotion, yet more ominous because of that, like the growling of a distant thunderstorm or an earthquake, letting you know you were in danger. "I just wanted to cover my ears. And my eyes. It was so scary, these cut people, and the blood and the smell. I needed to vomit too, but my mother was trying to find both of my brothers, so she just dragged me after her, breaking my wrist the way she held it. So I could not close my eyes or stop to vomit. Then the warriors caught us." The flow of the words stopped abruptly as if cut.

"Then what happened?" he asked, not wishing to hear, yet, somehow needing to know.

She swallowed, and he could feel her tensing by his side, although she had been anything but relaxed before.

"Then nothing," she said finally, her voice unnaturally low. "The warriors dragged her away. And… And after a while some people killed them and took me along, and we fled into the woods. And that's it. We came here."

The silence was so deep, he could hear the distant voices of the town behind their backs. Branches cracked in the woods, and the sound of the water trickling below their feet could have been calming but for her rigid, unsettling presence. It was strange to listen to the toneless voice telling him the story he had seen many times, had been a part of, but never from her side.

He remembered the towns they had taken, the villages they

had burned on the Tepanec side of the Great Lake. Yes, people would get cut in all sorts of ways, and women would be separated from their children, taken brutally and then either killed or tied to the poles for the slave traders to come and inspect. And children too, sometimes.

He shivered, remembering how he would shrug and go away. It was unpleasant to see, so he would just go. He never took a woman by force, but he never thought to prevent others from doing this.

"Did they..." He swallowed. "Did you see if they forced... forced your mother?"

If he thought she was tense or rigid before, he could feel her now turning into a stone.

"Yes," she said finally, her voice hardly audible, difficult to hear above the bubbling of the water.

His stomach turned as another thought hit him. "And you?"

She said nothing, and he almost breathed with relief. No, of course they would not. She must have been just a child back then.

"Yes." It came out even quieter than before, just a whisper really.

He felt it like a powerful blow in his stomach. For a heartbeat he was unable to breathe. But of course! It would explain her terrified reaction when she had run from him through the woods last night or when that lowlife he had fought grabbed her arm, telling them that she would stay to amuse them. Oh, he should have cut the bastard after all.

"I'm sorry," he said gruffly. "I'm sorry it happened."

Her voice cut the night sharply. "It happened more than three summers ago. I've forgotten all about it."

Oh no, you have not, he thought, admiring her courage, wishing he had never asked, her terrified face lingering in his memory, refusing to leave.

A gust of fresh wind brought along clouds. The moon disappeared, and for a while they were cast into an almost complete darkness.

He listened to the rustling of the bushes below their feet. The Lowlanders had done many bad things, and yet, he had been one of them for more than two summers. He fought alongside them, sharing their good moments and their hardships, forming fleeting friendships or rivalry, just like here in the Highlands, his hometown. Some people were good, some bad, some funny or grim, some took pleasure in being cruel, and some thought the side-effects of the war were an inevitable evil. Yet, there would always be wars and warriors. How could people solve their differences otherwise? And how would they feed the gods without a captured enemy?

"Anyway, that's not why I came looking for you," she said after a while in a clearer voice, back to her old self, unafraid and sincere.

"Why then?"

"That annoying old man was somewhat alone. His companions said your father was actually a good leader." She paused, and he began feeling better. "But then they agreed that maybe it was time to change the War Leader, anyway."

"That's what they said?" he repeated, his peacefulness gone once again.

She nodded, still observing the river. "And then, well, then someone said that they may try to get him through you."

He felt the air leaving his lungs all over again. "Through me?"

"Yes."

"How?"

She hesitated and in the resumed moonlight he could see her frowning, shutting her eyes for a heartbeat. "They said you are violent and angry. They said you could be easily provoked." Her voice died away gradually. "That's what they said."

"Well," he said slowly. "What did they propose to do about that?"

He could feel her shrugging. "Isn't it obvious?"

"No, it is not!" He fought his rising anger. "What does all of this have to do with my father?"

This time her voice rang softly, filled with compassion. "They said if you get in trouble, your father will try to help you out and then, you know…" Her words lingered in the air, uncomfortably real.

He clenched his fists to stop his hands from trembling.

"Why do they all assume that my father does what he does because of me?" he exclaimed through his clenched teeth. "He knows we will have to seek allies among our fallen enemy against the common threat. That's why he agreed to let Coyotl stay." He drew a deep breath. "Not because of me, even if they all think I'm at fault. I happened to bring the prominent Acolhua here, but had anybody else done that, the War Leader would have behaved the same way. To assume otherwise would be to belittle the great man he is. Yet, they all, even my mother, keep assuming that he is just indulging one of his sons. How stupid those people are. And how unappreciative. He led them for so many summers. Does it count for nothing?" He felt like crushing something. "They are all just ungrateful, filthy rats!"

She kept silent, and he was grateful for that. There was nothing to say, really. Some jealous people were after his father and his high position, while others just thought he was making a mistake. And his enterprising enemies were not above trying to get to the War Leader by any means, including through his hotheaded youngest son if need be.

He shivered, remembering the fight by the council building. Oh, but he hadn't even made his father's enemies wait. Had he killed this youth, he might have been offering those people a perfect opportunity. Oh, he was hopeless!

Glancing at the silent girl, he took in the gentleness of her silhouette, outlined clearly against the moonlit sky. How much courage for such a small, fragile thing. To throw herself between the two fighting people about to kill each other. To grab the arm with which he was holding the knife and not let it go even against his uncontrollable rage. She could have easily been killed, and the people around would only laugh, welcoming the additional entertainment.

"Thank you. Thank you for stopping this fight." He took a deep breath. "And thank you for coming to tell me about my father's enemies. You are truly brave."

She shrugged, smiling faintly, but the glance that she shot at him made him uneasy. There was a question in her eyes, a sort of a wary expectation.

"I have to go and talk to my father," he said, getting to his feet. "Where do you want me to take you in the meanwhile? Back to your place in the woods?"

She leaped to her feet and stood on the very edge of the cliff, eyeing him with those large, troubled eyes of hers.

"I don't know. I think it would be difficult to get there in the darkness. The moon will not help us there." She hesitated. "I'm going away tomorrow. I need to get things for the journey. Blankets and some clothes, and food. Can you help me with this?"

"Where are you going?"

"Back to my homeland."

He eyed her, puzzled. "But your village has been burned."

"There are other villages around our valley." She tossed her head. "I can't stay in Huexotzinco anyway now. Not after this."

"I could make sure no one attacks you anymore," he said, uncertain as to how he would do this.

Her face darkened. "It's not that. I'm not afraid of those filthy rats." She shrugged. "The man that was plotting against your father saw me. He knew I had listened to what he said."

He stared at her, wide-eyed. "Did he catch you eavesdropping? How did you get away?"

"I don't know. Somehow I slipped from his filthy paws, and then I ran all the way down to the river." She winced, brushing her palms against her upper arms. "It still hurts where he grabbed me. He was so angry, but scared too."

He bit his lower lip. "I can still make sure you are safe, somehow. I'll think of something. You don't have to run away."

"I want to," she said, her faint smile returning. "I have planned to do this since last autumn. I'll manage." She eyed him closely. "But you can help me prepare my journey. And also," her gaze dropped all of a sudden, "maybe we can find our way back to my place, and… and you can stay there again, like you did last night."

He watched her fingers playing with the rim of her gown, crushing the dusty, torn fringes.

"I can't. I have to go back and talk to my father." Unsettled by the flicker of hurt in her eyes, he frowned. "But I'll take you there now. Then I'll come tomorrow and bring you those things you need. The blankets and the food."

She peered at him, her lips clasped tight, eyes dark and somehow agitated. "Then I'll stay here and wait for you. I don't want to go back and be there alone. I don't think I will be safe there anymore, and… well, I'll wait for you here."

"Here?" He looked around, puzzled.

Her gaze did not leave his face, intense and almost agonizing. "Will you stay with me here?"

"What?"

"I… I just want you to stay," she stammered, the knuckles of her clasped palms whitening. "I… I thought you may want to…"

He took an involuntary step back, almost tripping off the low cliff. "No, I don't!" Flabbergasted, he stared at her. "How could you think that? You are just a child!"

"I'm not a child! I've seen fifteen summers."

"You don't look that old."

"I know, but I was born fifteen summers ago all the same." Her eyes darkened. "Also, I told you I was taken before."

Finding it hard to believe they were having this conversation, he shifted from one foot to the other. "There is a difference between being taken and making love."

"So you don't want to make love to me?"

"No! You still look too young and… and there are many reasons. You see, this is not how it's done."

She glared at him for a heartbeat, then turned away. "Oh well, then go."

Her thin arms wrapped around her shoulders, she stood there, small and forlorn, outlined clearly against the dark sky. The silence prevailed, interrupted by the rustling of the wind in the bushes behind their backs. He hesitated, fighting the urge to just turn around and leave.

"Listen," he said, coming closer, standing behind her, at a loss. "It is not something you should feel bad about. You are too young to understand it just yet."

"I know I'm not pretty," she whispered. "And not attractive like those other girls. I know that. It's just…" Her voice broke, and he could not understand the rest of her words.

Taken with compassion, he took hold of her trembling shoulders, turning her around, pressing her between his palms.

"It's not true. You are pretty. Very pretty even. Those other girls in the town, the ones who attacked you, they are just stupid, fat, useless rodents. I wouldn't touch them even if forced."

One hand under her chin, he made her look up, taking in the nicely defined cheekbones, the heart-shaped face narrowing toward the pointed chin, dominated by those dark oval eyes, enhanced by the shining tears. Dark, but not as dark as obsidian. The Texcocan goddess of the moon was also thin and angular and still well shaped, also wild and not-fitting, also only fifteen summers old. But there ended the similarities. This girl was not *her*.

"You are pretty and attractive. It's just that there are twenty and more reasons why I can't make love to you now. You will understand when you are older."

He could see her lips quivering, fighting a smile. Her eyes shone at him, suddenly powerful, making her look older, more of a woman. "You wouldn't touch any of those girls?"

"Oh, no! Especially not the fat, ugly bear you fought. Even if I would be forced not to touch a woman in my entire life, I'm telling you." Encouraged by her open delight, he grinned. "And with all this height and width she couldn't even take you. Because you are small and thin, but you have muscles, you run and climb all the time. One can see that. And you are a fighter."

Her body trembled with laughter, warm in his arms. Through the holes in her gown her skin felt smooth and creamy, inviting his palms to explore farther. The unreserved smile made her face look softer, more womanly. Now he noticed that her lips were full and well defined in the moonlit darkness. He knew he should go away. Yet, it would make her feel bad again.

"So, what girls would you touch without being forced?" she asked, eyes shining.

He shrugged, unsettled by the reaction of his body, fighting the urge to pull her closer.

"Was there a girl that you loved to make love to?"

While he was pondering his answer, she shifted closer. He didn't notice her moving, but somehow her body was pitted against his, her face beaming at him from below, eyes innocent and smiling, not intense and not dark anymore.

"You ask too many questions," he said, watching her lips as they parted slightly, as if expectant of his answer.

She just peered at him, and somehow, he knew it would be all right to taste those lips. Just a kiss, nothing more. They were so close anyway.

He felt her arms sneaking up, locking around his back, hurting the fresh bruises on it. Her kiss was artless, innocently simple. Still, it made his heart race, setting his body on fire.

She winced as his lips parted hers, and her body tensed.

"If you want to make love, you will have to trust me," he said, his voice low and difficult to recognize.

"I trust you," she whispered. "Please don't leave me just now."

Her arms tightened around him as her body pressed against his. He sensed it relaxing, and suddenly, it felt right to let go. She was a woman, or almost a woman, after all, and she had asked him to do it.

"Come," he said, propelling her toward the darkness of the trees, pleased with her quick, wordless reaction.

He didn't want to talk, suddenly trembling with impatience, the trees and the night and the star-sprinkled sky bringing back the wonderful memory. No, she was not the goddess of the moon, she was too small and too thin, and she felt and tasted differently; she even spoke a different tongue. Yet his body craved her now almost as much as it had craved *her*, the tall Acolhua princess. For three full summers, laying with occasional women, he hadn't felt anything like that, not even close.

CHAPTER 9

Coyotl stood on the dusty road, eyeing the narrowing path, hesitating. The stone house behind the patio looked quiet and deserted in the soft midmorning light.

He had never come so close to the dwelling of the War Leader, keeping a respectable distance since arriving at Huexotzinco. He knew he would not be allowed to stay without the consent of this formidable man, yet, until the previous day, he'd had no idea of the active support the man was issuing on his behalf.

Reassured, if still wary, he wouldn't dare to look up the company of the formidable leader even now but for his missing friend. Kuini had not come to sleep in his brother's house last night. Nothing out of the ordinary, yet this time Coyotl had expected him. They had much to discuss after their evening conversation, and he needed to hear what had transpired. After all, the Highlander had gone to talk to his father about the whole matter, and Coyotl, being directly involved, felt entitled to know what was decided.

He frowned, shaking his head. Kuini was the most loyal friend a man could have asked for, but his independent ways were sometimes a hindrance. The Highlander was impossible to predict or to try to coordinate any action with. He acted as if his course was always the best, and he never bothered to stop and check what the others were doing, curse his widely-spaced Tepanec eyes.

Watching the passersby uneasily, Coyotl shifted his weight from one foot to another. Should he enter and see if Kuini was in there, sleeping snugly after the difficult conversation with his sire on the night before? In this part of the morning the War Leader must be out already, so he, Coyotl, should be relatively safe in coming in.

Still pondering, he began walking the path. The silence was deep, encompassing. He took another long breath to calm his taut nerves. No one would be there, he promised himself. Probably not even Kuini, unless the Highlander was still fast asleep, which was not likely. Kuini was always up before the birds, as was appropriate for the ambitious warrior that he was. Yet, if not there, then where had the annoying hothead disappeared since the previous night?

Facing the half open screen, Coyotl peeked in, curious to inspect how a great leader lived. From the outside, this house looked no different than the others, although he would expect a prominent man to enjoy more luxury than his peers. It would not make sense otherwise…

His heart missed a beat, then threw itself wildly against his ribcage. The Leader of the Warriors squatted comfortably beside a low table, sipping from a plain-looking cup what seemed to be water and not the spicy *pulque* favored by the Highlanders. Before Coyotl could start deliberating about his next move, whether it was wiser to beat a hasty retreat or to move on with as much dignity as he could muster, the man raised his head. Expressionless, he watched Coyotl for a heartbeat, then nodded, gesturing the intruder to come in, neither hostile nor overly friendly.

Legs heavy, heart beating fast, Coyotl neared, hesitating again, finding it difficult to meet the man's gaze. He had happened to see the formidable leader on several occasions during his stay in Huexotzinco, and he had heard a lot about this man. They said he was a tough, ruthless leader and warrior when it came to politics and warfare; however, as a man the War Leader was reported to be easy-going, prone to laughter and fond of a pleasant pastime, never presuming to feel above his peers because of the duties he had been entrusted with.

Well, now the man did not look at peace with his world. Dark rings surrounded his eyes, and his lips were pressed tight, making the sun-burned, weathered face look older and grimmer.

"Well, Heir to the Texcoco throne, come and have a seat," the man finally said. "It's been some moons since you've arrived here, and I wish I'd had a chance to meet you personally sooner than that. Regretfully, the developments in your areas kept me quite busy."

Coyotl perched on the edge of the mat opposite to the War Leader, growing more uncomfortable with each passing moment. Frantically, he searched for something to say.

The man shrugged, then grinned, clearly making an effort to lighten up the atmosphere. "Although the Tepanecs took their time growing familiar with their newly acquired lands, didn't they?" He shrugged again. "I suppose, with their Empire encompassing the entire Great Lake now, they must have been too preoccupied to sniff around the conquered *altepetl*s." A twisted grin dawned. "Unlike the persistent Acolhua people, they seem not sure enough of themselves to venture into our mountains, not yet."

Coyotl swallowed, fighting the overwhelming urge to drop his gaze. He stared at the dark calmness of the large eyes, peering at him out of the long, narrow face, so atypical to the Highlanders and the Lowlanders alike. Kuini looked nothing like his father, he reflected randomly, licking his lips.

"I... I'm sorry that our people have been at war," he muttered. "I wish I could have done something about it."

The man nodded thoughtfully. "Oh, you could have, had you been able to inherit what was rightfully yours," he said quietly, as if talking to himself. "You are not an ordinary person. One could see that from the distance of a long bow shot and more. Your most unusual friendship with my son is only one of the indications. Both of you must be quite extraordinary youths to act the way you've acted." He shrugged again, then looked away. "I wish I could understand my son better."

"He worships you," said Coyotl, suddenly more at ease.

A skeptical glance was his answer. "I wouldn't be so sure about that."

"He came to talk to you last night, didn't he?" Coyotl

straightened his gaze, not afraid anymore. There was something about this man, something that made him relax, although he tried to curb the unfamiliar sensation. One couldn't trust a person after only a few sentences exchanged, even if one was still alive and relatively well thanks to this very same person.

The Leader studied his cup. "No, he did not."

"But he intended to. He left in order to do so."

"What did he want to talk about?"

Coyotl took a deep breath. "He happened to overhear what went on in the leaders' gathering. He worried about it, and he wanted to help." Hesitating under the suddenly concentrated gaze, he took a deep breath. "He wanted to let you know that we, he and I, we will go away in order to remove the problem my presence here is creating."

The dark gaze did not waver, but something flickered in the depths of the piercing eyes.

"Is that what he wanted to suggest? An interesting solution, although, I may have a better one." This time the eyes twinkled in amusement. "Where did he propose you two should go?"

"I don't know," said Coyotl, regretting disclosing the information. Under this man's amused gaze, Kuini's proposal sounded childish, too simplified, worthy of two youths and not two warriors, one of which was supposed to become an emperor. "Deeper into the Highlands, I would think," he added, feeling obliged to explain.

The man's grin widened. "Given the circumstances, this willingness to leave is most considerate of you two." He nodded, shaking his head, obviously still amused. "I appreciate it. But as I said, I may have a better solution."

Getting to his feet with the ease of a younger person, the leader went out of the room, leaving Coyotl to sit there, his nerves taut, pondering as to the nature of this "better solution." Would it include cutting out his heart on the altar of their mighty *Camaxtli* after all?

"Come to think of it," said his host, bringing back another decorated cup. "He did show up for a short while last night. I had company at the time, so, I suppose, he made sure to disappear as quickly as he could."

Grateful for the offered drink, although he still didn't like the overly spicy taste of the *pulque* – so much stronger than the delicate, well-brewed *octli* – Coyotl smiled.

"Back when we were children, before it all happened, before the war broke out." He cleared his throat. "Back then we would talk, and he would always say how his father was the great leader of the united clans and how no one could best him in anything. I know he is angry with you now, but I don't think he has stopped worshiping you."

The man's gaze deepened. "Yes, he came to discover some family secrets in the worst possible way. Still, his reaction was peculiar. When he went away, I assumed he would do something stupid, but I never imagined he would go as far as joining your father's war." Lips tight, the man shook his head. "To think of him fighting alongside our enemies, against more of our enemies. Inconceivable!"

"Our people don't have to be enemies."

"Don't they?" The gaze boring into him grew suddenly colder.

Coyotl shifted uneasily, clasping his palms together. "No," he said, gathering all the courage he possessed. "We don't need your lands, and you don't need ours. Our people can co-exist with no fighting. We have enough enemies from across the Great Lake to keep our gods properly fed. The Tepanecs would see to that, would supply us with enough captives to sacrifice on our altars, the Lowlanders and the Highlanders alike. The war against them would take summers upon summers, and in the meanwhile, our people will grow to know each other, the way Kuini and I grew to know each other after we first met, nearly ten summers ago." He paused for breath, then went on hurriedly, suddenly at ease and anxious to say that. "We were just children, and we punched each other the way children do, because he said the *calmecac* boys were soft, and I said things about the savages. But something had interrupted and, well, we stopped and started to talk. And then meet occasionally."

He recalled that day as if it had happened only a few dawns ago, the scorching heat of the sun blazing upon his favorite Tlaloc hill, his thirst, his fear, his curiosity. It had happened on the same day his father, the Emperor, had put aside his Tepanec Chief Wife to favorite the Aztec one, Coyotl's mother, starting his rebellion against the Tepanecs. So much had changed since that day. Now his father was dead and Texcoco conquered, taken by the Tepanecs, to be tossed disdainfully as a prize to the traitorous Aztecs. His desperation welled, but he pushed it aside, concentrating on the foreign-looking face of the Warriors' Leader, meeting the dark eyes once again, liking the way the man watched him calmly, as if seeing through him, as if not disapproving.

"And that's what would happen to our people. When they would take the time to know each other, they wouldn't want to war against one another. They would be friends, and we would fight together, against the Aztecs and the Tepanecs. They would have made great allies and friends had the things been different."

The gaze of the man lost its intensity, turned amused once again. "This is an interesting vision. But weren't the Aztecs your people's worthwhile allies and friends as well?"

"The Aztecs betrayed us! They did not come to our aid when we needed them most. They watched, amused and indifferent, when we struggled against the mighty Tepanecs, and then they turned around and joined our enemies, tipping the scales." He fought for breath, his rage sudden and overwhelming. "Because of them, we have lost. Their despicable betrayal sealed my people's fate. I will not forgive those people even if I live ten times twenty summers and more!"

The man nodded again, reaching for a flask. He poured two cups and offered Coyotl one. The thick beverage smelled spicy, but Coyotl didn't mind this time. Drinking thirstily, he relished the burning sensation running down his throat, warming it, making him feel alive again.

"I see you harbor much anger, young man," said the old warrior calmly, his smile surprisingly well meaning. "An understandable thing, given the circumstances. Yet, it seems that the Aztecs might be your means to return to the Texcoco's throne. Ridiculous, I know," he added, his smile widening against Coyotl's gaping face. "And seemingly impossible. However, you may have a chance to get back to rule Texcoco and your Acolhua people."

The man paused, sipping from his cup.

"I wish to make something clear," he said finally, his face losing its amiable expression. Now it was the War Leader of the United Clans speaking. "I would never help your people get your Texcoco back. They were our relentless enemies for more summers than our elders can remember. All those lands down to the Great Lake shores, the *altepetl* of Texcoco included, once belonged to the Chichimecs. Those were our lands! Until the Tepanecs came in force, shoved our people aside, taking Texcoco and the Lowlands for the benefit of their Acolhua cousins. It happened a long time ago, but my people did not forget." He raised his hand, stopping anything Coyotl might have tried to say in protest. "I'm not bringing it up to make you feel bad. Your Acolhua people received this gift, and I'm sure they were grateful at the time. Even though their gratitude did not last for more than a few generations. Your father rebelled against the Tepanecs, and he lost. So now, here you are, living among the enemies of your people, coming to know them as you so eloquently stated."

The amused half grin was back, accompanied by the twinkling eyes this time.

"Now, I'll tell you why I think it might be wise to help you. I know the Tepanecs; I know them quite well. The other leaders think the Tepanecs may be better neighbors than your Acolhua people were. Since taking Texcoco and the provinces, they have kept to the Lowlands, not venturing near our mountains. However, I think my peers are wrong. The Tepanecs won't stay low for more than a few more summers. They will start raiding our settlements soon enough, as soon as they begin feeling comfortable on this side of the Great Lake.

"I don't know if my son told you, but I was born in Azcapotzalco, to a very prominent, outstanding man, the Chief Warlord and, later, the closest Adviser of Tezozomoc himself. When I left, I was already a warrior, about your age, en-route to joining the elite forces of the blue-cloaks." The gaze of the man deepened, lost its concentration, wandering the mists of the past.

"I left for various reasons, but none of them had anything to do with anger. I didn't feel bad about my country-folk, although by that time Tezozomoc was being hideously unfair to my father. My whole family left Azcapotzalco, never to return, each heading his own way and for his own personal reasons."

An ironic smile softened the man's hard features, made him look younger.

"I drifted here for all sorts of wrong causes, like only a youth of your age would do, following a pretty face. I didn't plan to stay. Yet, the Highlands have worked their magic on me. I stayed and turned into a highlander. I forgot my past. I did not remember it anymore. Azcapotzalco did not exist for me. I didn't bother to tell my children they were half Tepanecs, although I taught them to speak the Nahuatl of the Lowlands, so they could understand the enemy better." The man shrugged, his soft, mirthless smile widening. "I do understand Kuini's anger. What Highlander would want to discover one day that he was half a Tepanec. You wouldn't like it either, I bet."

The dark eyes concentrated, focusing, and Coyotl shook off the dreamy sensation.

"Yes," he said, still under the spell of the story, feeling closer to the man than he had ever felt to his own father, the distant Emperor. "I would feel strange had my father told me I was half a Chichimec."

The Leader's laughter rolled between the stone walls. "Oh, yes. This is a good comparison." He slapped his palm against the table, still laughing. "You are a sharp boy. You may make a good emperor, after all."

Coyotl's mood darkened. "I won't have a chance," he muttered.

"Well, it still remains to be seen." The man sobered. "Which brings me to the beginning of our conversation. I don't want the Tepanecs on our side of the Great Lake. It will take them time to understand our balance of forces, but, in the end, they'll attempt to climb our mountains and lay waste to our settlements." The rough, brown palms rested on the table, coarse, determined, and lethal. "I may try to help you get your *altepetl* and its provinces back. Whether I'll manage it is another question. Given the current situation, I may not be in a position to help when the time comes. Yet, before I do anything, I will have to know if I can trust you to keep your end of the bargain." The penetrating gaze bore into Coyotl, suddenly difficult to bear.

Coyotl licked his lips. "What will be my side of the bargain?"

"Isn't that obvious?" The large eyes twinkled again, but not friendly this time.

Coyotl swallowed. "Oh, well, of course. When I'm an emperor no Acolhua warrior would come near the Highlands. The people of the Lowlands and your united clans will never war again."

The thoughtful gaze did not waver. "It is easier to say than to achieve. Do you realize that?"

"I do." Coyotl took a deep breath. "I've been helping my father even before the first Tepanec invasion. I know how difficult it is to run a great *altepetl* and its provinces, to make people obey. Even the warlords and advisers needed to be reminded of their duties, of their commitments from time to time." He straightened his gaze. "But I will manage to be obeyed. I'll choose the right people to serve me. My warlords will know better than to try to argue, to even think of nearing the lands of the people who had helped me get my Texcoco back. We will not war on each other as long as I live."

The warrior's gaze softened as another of his amused grins flashed. "Well, then it boils down to getting you back onto the Texcoco throne." The grin disappeared. "Not a small undertaking. And it'll take more than a few summers to achieve. Do you realize that?"

Coyotl's heart fell, and it must have reflected upon his face as the man shook his head, his grin spreading back. "Oh, you didn't think I'd just gather my warriors and roll down the First Pass right toward Texcoco, did you?"

"No, of course not!" said Coyotl, his jaw tightening. It was precisely how he had imagined it would happen. *How else would they get him back to Texcoco?*

Now the man laughed outright. "Patience, boy. Patience is the most important quality in a successful ruler. Your father lacked it.

That's why he lost. You see, he should have waited with this rebellion of his. Tezozomoc is a very old man. He cannot walk our Fifth World for much longer. Your father should have waited until this particular ruler embarked upon his journey through the realm of the dead."

Where had he heard this already? wondered Coyotl, only a tiny part of his mind dwelling on the question. The rest was washed with a wave of indignant rage. *Why was he so transparent? Why did this man see through him so easily?*

"How would the death of Tezozomoc change anything?" he asked as calmly as he could, mostly to take the attention off his blunders. "The Tepanec Empire would still be there, with all their multitude of warriors, lands and resources."

"Oh, but they would lack a good, experienced leadership, which makes an enormous difference. It changes everything, Netzahualcoyotl. It takes a great leader to carve an empire. But it requires a man just as great to run it, to maintain it, to make it work. A poor leader can see a well-run empire crashing down around him, and he would never understand what happened." The thoughtful gaze resting on Coyotl was as dark as a pond on a moonless night. "Tezozomoc will be dead in a few summers. Then we'll see what's happening. We'll see how his successor will handle this huge empire he'll receive. Then we'll act accordingly."

Coyotl forced his palms into calmness. "Yes, you are right. Of course, you are right. Thank you," he added, straightening his gaze. "Thank you for everything. I appreciate your willingness to help, but more than that, I appreciate your patience with me, and your advice. I will try to learn much from you in the summers to come."

The man's smile widened, yet the twinkle was back.

"Oh, yes, I'm sure you would have learned much, given a chance. You are a smart youth and very observant. But you won't have this chance." He laughed, while Coyotl struggled to regain his composure, desperate to banish the stunned expression off his face. "What? Did you think you would live here in peace, hunting and fooling around with local girls until it's time to roll down our mountains in force? Oh no, Future Emperor. You'll have to work, to work hard. You'll have to get things ready for my warriors to go and take your Texcoco back. Don't tell me you are afraid of hard work."

"No, I'm not," mumbled Coyotl, hating the acute sensation of helplessness. "I'll do whatever it takes."

"Well, then let me explain the situation to you. In the Lowlands people don't know what's happening. They don't know where you are. They have no idea if the Emperor's heir is dead or alive. So, first of all, they have to discover you are alive and well, and that your spirit is not broken. The Acolhua people have to see the fine, young man who was supposed to become their next emperor." A rough palm came up, extending one finger. "That's the first thing – Acolhua people coming to all sorts of ideas all by themselves. Now," another finger came up, "the Tepanecs. They also should know about your existence. This would be a more difficult task. You would have to convince them that you are harmless, completely harmless. You would have to let them know that the only thing you crave is to live quietly somewhere around the Lowlands. They won't let you go back to Texcoco. Not right away. But eventually they might, if convinced of your harmlessness; and your usefulness as well."

"Do I go down there then?" asked Coyotl, his mouth dry. It didn't make any sense, yet the man in front of him seemed so wise. There had to be a reason for his proposal.

The Warriors' Leader shook his head vigorously. "No, of course not. You'd be put to death quietly and efficiently. Or maybe with great pomp. Depends on Tezozomoc's mood."

"Then how?"

"You'll need someone influential and in a good stance with the Tepanecs to intercede on your behalf. Someone who would be willing to be responsible for your behavior until the Tepanec Emperor is convinced by your performance."

Coyotl stared at the narrow, weathered, wrinkled face, refusing to ask any more questions. He had made a complete fool of himself so far, promising to be a good emperor then proceeding to show how simple and unsophisticated his thinking was.

The amused smile playing upon the man's lips made him

understand that he did not need to utter the question to make matters worse. "You'll have to go to Tenochtitlan."

"What? Tenochtitlan? Why?" He brought his hands to his burning cheeks and didn't care how silly he might look anymore. "The treacherous Aztecs betrayed us. What will I do in Tenochtitlan?"

The man nodded thoughtfully. "Yes, they did betray you last summer. There were all sorts of political implications that led to it, not all of them pure. Their Palace is a nest of wild bees. Not a safe place to be around, especially if you are someone of importance."

The thought of Iztac-Ayotl hit him like a fist in the stomach, making him fight for breath. She was sent there, distraught and unwilling, sacrificed for nothing, and she was still there, now the Emperor's widow. If he went to Tenochtitlan he might see her there, if she was alive and well.

He heard the man in front of him talking and concentrated with an effort. "My brother told the Acolhua Emperor to wait with his rebellion. Pity your father's ears weren't open to a piece of a good advice."

"Your brother?" asked Coyotl, trying to understand. *When had the Texcoco Emperor conversed with important highlanders?*

"Yes. Tenochtitlan's Chief Warlord had advised your father to wait until Tezozomoc's death." The man's grin widened. "Oh, don't tell me you didn't know. After what happened three summers ago my family connections in Tenochtitlan seemed to have become a common knowledge."

But of course! How could he have forgotten it? Coyotl bit his lips, angry with himself. He remembered Kuini telling him this whole story on their way here, with the fires of Huexotla gleaming behind their backs. He remembered his friend's handsome face twisted with rage, his prominent eyes flashing as he related his family's surprising history, the way he had come to discover it, about his father and about that Aztec Warlord. Kuini's uncle, for gods' sake!

He remembered the Aztec well, too. The arrogant, annoyingly self-assured man, presuming to advise the Emperor of Texcoco in front of his subjects, telling the mighty ruler his politics were a mistake. Oh, how appalled he, Coyotl, had been. How enraged. How the Emperor and his advisers were left speechless at such effrontery. And yet, the Aztec Warlord had been right all along. And this leader of the Highlanders was right as well. Two very wise men. And brothers. Unbelievable!

"Tenochtitlan's young emperor is just a boy, reported to be a nice person with a strong sentiment for his Acolhua cousins. Yes, under his rule Tenochtitlan betrayed Texcoco. Under the rule of Huitzilihuitl, the Aztec island struggled to stay neutral, trying to maintain the fragile balance in not angering their overlords while not betraying their allies. It's said that upon receiving the Tepanec request for an active participation, Huitzilihuitl was downcast, stating that he could not, would not, do this. They say that a few days before his untimely death he had decided to join the struggle of the Acolhua people." The man shrugged. "Too bad he had died. Such a healthy man that had seen less than twice twenty summers."

Coyotl swallowed. "Was his death hastened?"

"There are people who think so, yes. His Empress, Tezozomoc's favorite daughter, must have been relieved."

Clasping his palms tight, Coyotl stared at the impassive face of the Highlander Leader, taking in the calm wisdom and the strange glint to the dark eyes. "So, she is the one to rule Tenochtitlan now?"

"Well, technically, it's the boy, Huitzilihuitl's son, who is the Emperor. But yes, being a child of a little more than half twenty summers, this boy receives his mother's guidance with gratitude. And it's not that Huitzilihuitl has no other sons, some of them are your age and more fitting to inherit. Tlacaelel, his oldest, for example, is a very capable young man, a good warrior, a good person. I wonder for how much longer this particular youth will walk our Fifth World."

Coyotl's mouth was so dry he found no relief in licking his lips. "Then what shall I do in Tenochtitlan, except trying to avoid their attempts to hasten my death?"

"Well, there are many Mexica people who do not approve of their Emperor's, or their Empress's, policies. These people think

Tenochtitlan should not be turned into yet another Tepanec province. It's happening rapidly, you see? Soon this island will not be just another tributary; it would be an inseparable part of the Tepanec Empire with no independence whatsoever. There are many Aztecs who see what's happening and who would love to prevent that." The man nodded. "I hear things may change."

"How? The Empress must be very powerful. She won't let anyone influence her policies."

A smile dawned, a thoughtful, mirthless grin. "What happened to her husband can happen to anyone."

Coyotl gasped, then clenched his teeth in an attempt to control his expression, embarrassed by his own naivety, his lack of control.

"It takes one courageous, determined, influential person to do what she did. Someone who would not be afraid to lose, and who would have everything to gain should he succeed."

"Me? You want me to do this?" He found it hard to form those words, his mouth numb, heart going quiet as if it had stopped beating for good.

"No, of course not." The sudden laughter of the old warrior was hearty, if inoffensive. "Yet, you may be able to help, somehow. Or maybe just enjoy the fruits of this person's deed." The man's palms rested against the crude surface of the table as he leaned forward. "In any case, you should be there, making friends with the Emperor. He is a nice boy from what I hear, so it won't be a difficult task. You have a knack for connecting with people. While watching you, I was impressed with the way you handled my countryfolk. Many accept and like you these days because of what you are, despite your origins and your family ties. It's an admirable quality. It helped me to convince some of our leading people that you could be a good choice of an emperor to rule the Lowlands."

Coyotl took a deep breath. "I will not disappoint you and your people," he said gruffly.

"I should hope not." The man straightened up. "Well, now, let us discuss the details. When you reach Tenochtitlan, you will seek an audience with my brother, the former Chief Warlord. You won't have difficulty finding him. He is well known in Tenochtitlan." The leader's grin widened. "He is not a person to live modestly. He takes whatever life is willing to offer, so he is very influential, even these days, when he is not the Chief Warlord anymore. I suppose my son would wish to accompany you, which might make it easier for you. Let him handle the Warlord. Those two got along quite well in the past." The smile disappeared. "My brother will help you connect with the right people."

"I... I don't think the Warlord would wish to help me." Coyotl swallowed. "I met him before. We didn't get along and, well, after all that happened in Texcoco, with my father and all..."

He watched the man filling their cups with more drink, grateful for the distraction.

"He'll help you. He would be the one suggesting this had he known you were hiding here in our mountains. As it was, I thought of it first."

Coyotl gasped. "Why?"

"He doesn't like what's going on in Tenochtitlan. He may not like you personally, although I doubt that, given the fact that you were a mere youth of no importance when you two met." The gaze of the War Leader flickered above his cup. "He is not concerned with your personal well being, whether he likes you or not. He is concerned with what is going on in Tenochtitlan, and he may see the way to use you, for the benefit of you both." The man's eyes softened. "Remember this, Netzahualcoyotl. People don't have to like you in order to help you. Most people will help you in the way they can benefit from it, and they'll do it better than those who would want to do something for you personally. You will learn to use people too, and it's a good thing." The cup made a hollow sound upon the surface of the wooden table. "Different people's interests are often going along with each other. People are using each other to achieve their goals. There is nothing wrong with that. The trick is to let people use you only when it suits you and helps you with your own goals, but not in any other case." The man's gaze concentrated, growing sterner but also warmer. "I sent him word some time ago and I hoped to wait for his answer. He may have better suggestions. Yet, as the situation looks here now, you may wish to go to Tenochtitlan with no further delay. I may not be able to protect you here any longer." He shrugged. "So my son's idea is not a bad one. All you needed was a direction and now you have it."

Coyotl's heart squeezed, detecting the sadness and the flicker of pain in the depths of the dark eyes before the man's gaze shifted, brushing past the table and the cups, the lines around the pursed mouth deepening.

"I'm deeply sorry for being a cause of your trouble. I wish I could do something to prevent it, to make people understand."

The eyes concentrated and the creases around the generous mouth smoothed. "Oh, I'm not finished yet," the old leader said with a laugh. "I won't be cast aside that easily, neither me nor my far-fetched ideas." The confident grin widened. "I know I'm right about you and about the Aztecs and the Tepanecs. We will have to fight together with your people. We should have done it in the first place. After the Tepanecs are thrown back, we can reverse to our Flowery Wars as far as I'm concerned. But for a short period of time, we will have to forget our differences."

"We will not reverse to our Flowery Wars," said Coyotl, putting his cup back. "We will find other people to fight and other captives to sacrifice. Texcoco and Huexotzinco will never war again."

The War Leader smiled lightly, but in the depths of his eyes Coyotl could see a flicker of satisfaction. "That will be up to you, young man. Now go, find my son, and you two had better start preparing your journey."

Easier said than done!

Irritated more than amused, Coyotl made his way up the river bank, wondering. Where in the name of the Underworld could Kuini have disappeared?

Unwilling to search through the town that may now be full of hostile or suspicious people, he headed for the river, craving the privacy the surrounding woods provided. He needed to think, to think hard.

Was it possible to get Texcoco back after all? He had never allowed such spark of hope enter his mind. His life as the future Acolhua Emperor was in the past. It was all lost, and after the difficult winter, he had come to grips with this thought, forcing himself to accept the bitter reality of his people's defeat. He would never rule Texcoco and its provinces. He would never live as an Acolhua person again. Yet, he had a great friend and his friend's people to build a new life with. He was better off than many of his former subjects. And yet now…

The midday sun warmed the air, and he offered his face to its caressing touch. Was it truly possible? The scheme the Warriors' Leader had come up with was wild, far-fetched, incredibly complicated, yet it did make perfect sense coming from the lips of this prominent, undeniably wise man. The man and his advice could be trusted.

However, the Aztec Warlord and other Tenochtitlan's dwellers were a different story. The Aztecs had done nothing but betray his, Coyotl's, people, now enjoying the fruits of their despicable betrayal. Why would they wish to help him? Why would they wish to change their policies now?

His legs took him up the riverbank without him noticing, but as he reached the familiar clearing he woke from his daydreams, the pictures of the previous afternoon invading his memory, pushing the other thoughts aside. Would she come here today? They had agreed to meet here. Or had they? After that stormy meeting with Kuini, he doubted the angry girl would ever show up again. A pity. He grinned, thinking how pleasant it would be to spend his last afternoon in the Highlands in this way.

Back up on the high riverbank, he strained his gaze, eyeing the forested areas beneath his feet. Where was the wild Highlander now? Why would he disappear like that without saying a word? He had gone to talk to his father, but now here they were, settled to go, with Coyotl doing the father-son conversation instead of his friend, reassuring the powerful War Leader that his son still thought the world of him despite acting quite the opposite.

He cursed silently, then listened. Branches creaked at a considerable distance, and the rustling of the bushes made an impression of someone hurrying up the forested path. At last!

Coyotl turned around, then froze, gasping. Iso, disheveled and dressed in a simple robe with none of her usual decorative jewelry, burst out of the bushes adorning the cliff.

"Thank all the gods you are here," she cried out, leaning forward, hands propped against her thighs, busy catching her breath.

Coyotl just stared, unable to take his eyes off her lovely face, now swollen on one side, displaying a blackish ring around one of her eyes. Her lower lip was split too, although the brownish crust did not seem to be fresh.

"What happened?" he called, coming back to his senses, leaping toward her, catching her by her shoulders, although she did not seem in need of support. "Who did this to you?"

She looked up, and there was an unpleasant spark to her eyes. "Don't worry about me, worry about yourself."

"What?"

"My man. He came back yesterday, and he wasn't happy with me being out the whole day."

Coyotl felt like taking a step back. With an effort he made himself remain still, not taking his supporting hands off her shoulders.

"Did he beat, beat you bad?"

She shrugged. "He was angry. You know how men get when they are jealous." Raising her eyebrows, she freed herself from his grip. "He knows it was you, so you better take yourself off for half a moon or so. He is on his way to Huexotzinco."

Heart beating fast, Coyotl struggled to appear calm. "How he find, how find out?"

She shrugged and there was coldness to her eyes now. "There is just so much pain that I can take. I didn't want him to ruin my appearances for good." She stood his glaring gaze. "I don't have to cover for you. I owe you nothing! Also, I did come here to warn you, so don't you look at me like that. You are to blame for this entire mess."

He cursed in Nahuatl, knowing better than to argue.

"What are you mumbling in that annoying tongue of yours?" she asked suspiciously.

"Nothing." He looked back at her without his previous affection. Still, her swollen cheek made him feel bad. "So, now what?"

"So, now nothing. Go away. Make sure to stay away for some time. Hope this scandal dies down without much fuss." She turned around abruptly. "I have to go." Another glance over her shoulder, this time sparkling with a hint of amused affection. "It was nice knowing you, Lowlander Emperor."

He listened to her dying footsteps, his heart beating fast. Then he remembered. Kuini! He had to find his friend in a hurry. They better leave as soon as they could.

CHAPTER 10

Kuini woke to the mild caress of the early sun. Atypically for him, he didn't spring to his feet, ready to start the day, but lay there lazily, not bothering to open his eyes.

It was such a strange, unfamiliar feeling. He, who had always woken up before the birds, since he could remember himself. An admirable trait in a man, a warrior, a hunter. The only admirable trait he had. All the rest were frowned upon.

Well, this time he had also woken when the night had began turning gray, remembering all the things he was supposed to do through the previous night. He had to talk to his father, then start preparing his and Coyotl's journey, finding a suitable destination, gathering the things they might need.

However, now there was the girl. He had to take care of her as well. Such a small, vulnerable thing could not be allowed to wander alone through the entire Tlaxcala Valley. Gods knew who were roaming their hills and mountains these days.

He grinned, remembering the way they had arrived in her cozy improvised semblance of a home. The spontaneous lovemaking on the river bank did not go well. Of course it did not. How could it? She was frightened and tense, so rigid and cold in his arms, his excitement had evaporated. Yet, she protested and tried to make him take her anyway. It was as if she were trying to prove something, to herself maybe, or to anyone else.

He had told her to forget it, but could not leave her there so downcast upon the riverbank. So they had gone all the way through the woods toward her makeshift home, walking in silence, each in their own frustrated thoughts. It would take him half a night to reach his father now, and, of course, no one would be awake and waiting by then.

However, the moon shone brightly and enticingly when they reached the cozy privacy of her improvised dwelling, and when she tried to make him stay, he hesitated, suddenly not finding it that necessary to return to the town tonight. Despite her bruised face and her torn, muddied clothes, she looked nicely sweet in the generous moonlight, attractive in her own wild way.

She piled up all the blankets she had to make his bed as soft as she could, and he smiled at her, appreciating her efforts. The desire was back, not as intense as in the woods, but cozy and intimate, as if he had known this place and this girl for summers, as if he had owned them both.

Seeing the look in his eyes and the smile, she tensed again and even began to protest, but he brushed her arguments aside, making her lie down beside him. Even though very thin, she was built prettily, he found out, removing her gown. Well shaped, curving in all the right places, her body looked especially enticing in the dim moonlit corner of their private world, but he curbed his impatience, taking her only when she was relaxed and ready to receive him. Only when she clung to him, murmuring in contentment, did he let the wave of excitement sweep him, make the world around them disappear, dissolve in the mists of divine pleasure, the place he had not managed to reach since that night in the Texcoco Palace more than three summers ago. This girl was not the goddess of the moon, but she was some forest spirit, oh yes, unlike the rest of the mortal women he had enjoyed on occasion.

And now, letting the caressing sun wake him, he smiled, not in a hurry to open his eyes. She was not cuddled beside him, like when he had awoken for the first time before dawn, but he could hear her moving about, tending the fire, judging by the lulling crackling of branches.

So, what do you do with her now? he asked himself, opening his eyes for just a fraction. He could hear her light footsteps coming in, lingering, hesitating beside him.

The answer presented itself readily. *You take her along and make sure she gets to whatever town or village around the Tlaxcala Valley she would like to settle in.* They would have to go deeper into the Highlands anyway now, and this direction was as good as any. Then, after settling her wherever she liked, he and Coyotl could decide on the best course of action, whether to go back to the Lowlands, to ambush the Tepanecs the way he had done a few days ago, or to do something else, as violent and as useful.

But for Coyotl, he knew, he would go to his uncle in Tenochtitlan. He sighed. Too bad it could not be done. The Aztec Warlord would be glad to see him, making sure his nephew got accepted into any warriors' force he liked.

She still stood above him as he opened his eyes, her face pretty and clean, adorned by the long, wet, neatly combed hair, sparkling with thousands drops of water. Fresh and extremely appealing, she gazed at him, smiling uncertainly, as expectant as a child promised a treat.

He smiled back at her, then stretched and sat up.

"Have you slept well?" she asked, not attempting to sit beside him.

"Oh, yes. Better than the night before even."

That made her giggle.

"I wish I could make a good morning meal for you," she said. "As it is, I have only some berries and things." She frowned. "It is too early for even the earliest corn."

"Do you grow things around here?" he asked, enjoying the sight of her.

"Yes, of course. I have some plants here. I'll be sorry to leave them behind." Her eyes lit as uncertainty left them. "I grow plants here, good useful plants."

Liking the way her cheeks colored, he caught her hand. "Well, it doesn't matter. I've been so hungry since yesterday that I've grown used to it. But I can think of a better way of spending the morning."

She gasped as he pulled her closer, making her stumble and fall on top of him. Her eyes were enormous in the sudden paleness of her small, heart-shaped face.

"What? Again?" she whispered, the uncertainty flooding back.

"Of course. Don't you want it?"

"I... yes, of course. It's just..."

She looked so confused and unsettled, it made him laugh. "Oh well, next time," he said, releasing her.

He began to get up, but she clung to him with surprising strength.

"No, no, of course we do it now," she said, suddenly back in control. "I want it, too. I was just surprised."

But again her body was tense, and it took him an effort to make her relax. Yet, it had been worth the trouble, he decided later, sprawling on his back, at peace with the world once again, watching the sun climbing up the cloudless sky. He wished he could spend the whole day here.

It was already well past midmorning when he hurried back toward Huexotzinco, his stomach churning with hunger, but his spirits high. A quick conversation with his father, then with Coyotl, and then they'd be ready to leave, maybe even tonight. And if not, then tomorrow, which would give him another night to spend with this strange but exciting girl.

From the high cliff he could see the whole town, sprawling upon the surrounding hills, peaceful in this time of the day, with most of its citizens out in the fields or in the woods, farming or hunting. A group of women knelt on a distant shore, picking blankets and gowns from diminishing piles of clothes.

When he noticed a figure hurrying down the hill in the direction of Huexotzinco, the swaying of the cloak and the outline of the sword upon its girdle unmistakable, he smiled. Perfectly on time. Hastening his steps, he took a shortcut, jumping down the rocks, knowing those hidden paths by heart.

What was Coyotl doing out there in the woods? he asked himself, then grinned once again. The girl. That cheeky girl with a good memory. Had his lusty friend went to enjoy her one more time?

Before turning back toward the more conventional road, he glanced down the cliff once again. The figure with the cloak was still visible, walking purposely, paces long and hurried. Yet, now Kuini's eyes detected a movement down the same trail. Still at a considerable distance, three men sneaked along the wide path, moving carefully as if unwilling to be detected.

Breath caught, he watched them for a heartbeat, taking in their cautious steps, like that of hunters, and the long clubs they carried. Another heartbeat, and he was charging down the rocks, his heart beating fast. Those people were following his friend, of that he was sure. They may have been following him for some time, or maybe they had just spotted him, but whatever were their intentions, they were closing on him now. Three people, armed with clubs against one man, a good warrior with an obsidian sword, but still only one man, and a foreigner into the bargain.

Slipping on the steep rocks, jumping over gaping cracks, Kuini forgot all about the wonderful morning and his plans. Oh, but of course there were people who wanted the highborn Lowlander dead. Plenty of those! He should have guarded his friend better, should not have left him to his own devices. He was so selfish.

His feet slipped more than once over the traitorous cliff with no path, but miraculously, he managed to catch himself every time he should have fallen, risking breaking his limbs. He would be of no help to Coyotl if injured, yet he could not take the normal path. He would never reach them in time.

The last jump was high, and he felt its impact in his lower back, landing upon the same trail, now completely abandoned. He didn't waste his time checking the signs, but ran down the narrow road as if a pack of hungry wolves were after him. Praying he would reach them in time, he untied his sword as he ran.

The road turned, and, with the town already in sight, he saw them, all four of them, with Coyotl pressed against the rock, grim but unafraid, his sword out, and the other three forming half a circle around him. A formidably large warrior stood closer than the rest, talking rapidly, spitting with rage.

Bursting upon them, Kuini halted abruptly, returning their stares, desperate to catch his breath. The other two stepped forward in unison, blocking his way. Kuini paid them no attention, staring at the broad face of their leader, trying to read through the anger that twisted the prominent features. What was his game? The intensity of the man's rage seemed strange, inappropriate. It felt like he had something personal against Coyotl. A family killed by Acolhua warriors?

The silence lasted for only a heartbeat.

"Go away, son of the War Leader," growled the man. "This matter has nothing to do with you."

Studying the slightly familiar, broad features, Kuini took a deep breath, striving to sound calm. He had seen this warrior somewhere, although the man was clearly not from Huexotzinco.

"I'm not going anywhere. You have no right to attack him, anymore than you have the right to attack me. He lives in Huexotzinco, and his origins are not of your concern." Pleased with his surprisingly calm voice, he glared at the man, but part of his attention was on the other two warriors, noticing the impatience of their poses and the glances they shot at their leader.

"I told you to go away, boy," repeated the man, his voice low, still in seeming control. "I have every right to kill the filthy Acolhua. I would take a great pleasure in killing you as well. I'm sure you knew all about what your excrement-eating friend did. But for the sake of your brother, I will let you go." The dark eyes went flat. "Now run away. This is your last chance."

Oh, now he remembered. But of course. He had seen this man in Nihi's house from time to time, two formidable hunters, friendly rivals and peers.

"You can't kill him," he repeated, feeling silly. "The council of the elders won't have it."

One of the other two warriors, a spare man with a scar crossing his cheekbone, let out a neigh of derisive laughter. "Stop blabbering, you lowlanders' lover. Go back to your losers. Go and find yourself another filth-eating Acolhua." He took a step, halting next to Kuini. "Or better yet, stay there for good, wild boy. This town was better off without you embarrassing it time after time."

The wave of familiar rage came forcefully, but this time Kuini fought it, remembering what the girl had said. They were trying to provoke him into killing someone, to use it later against his father.

He took a deep breath, his stomach churning, chest hurting.

Oh, how he craved to kill the insolent lowlife.

Before he could say anything, he heard Coyotl's voice, low and calm, well in control. "So, you go fight or talk?" demanded the Texcocan loudly, addressing the leader, the challenge in his voice unmistakable.

Finding it difficult to believe his ears, Kuini turned in time to see Coyotl stepping forward, his sword clasped tightly in both hands. The heir to the Texcoco throne had come to know their tongue well, he reflected randomly, trying to slam his mind into working.

The tall leader whirled at his opponent. "Oh yes, filthy Acolhua. I'm going to fight, and I'm going to make you suffer before you die."

Coyotl didn't wince, didn't take a step back. Jaw clenched, eyes blazing, he faced his attacker, obviously as eager to engage. "You strong, beat women. No men. No warriors."

A club hissed, cutting the air, crashing against the cliff where Coyotl had been standing a heartbeat before.

"And you think the Texcocan scum can lay his dirty hands on the real warriors' women?" breathed the man, swinging his club once again.

Kuini blinked, trying to understand. "What is going on?" he mumbled, at a loss for a moment.

He saw Coyotl ducking another onslaught, briefly meeting his friend's eyes.

"You better go," he heard him saying in Nahuatl. "This is something I'm responsible for, and I have to face it myself." This time his sword blocked another attack, the hands of both men trembling, holding against the pressure.

Still stunned, Kuini felt the other warrior leaping toward him. Out of instinct, he jumped aside, but no club or knife tore the air. The man was not attacking him, not yet. He stared into the scarred face.

"What are they fighting about?" he asked.

The man laughed, baring his large yellowish teeth. "What do you think, wild boy? Did you two think Yoho wouldn't discover your dung-eating friend laying his filthy hands on his woman?"

"He what?"

The man took another step, now standing next to Kuini, the spike on his club sparkling viciously, returning the rays of the high noon sun. He could feel the *pulque* and some spicy foodstuff upon the man's breath. He wished he hadn't understood it right.

"Oh yes, lowlanders' lover. Your precious friend took Yoho's woman, more than once, so the rumor has it. The stupid rat must have been thinking he is still an emperor, and that he could do as he pleased." He laughed into Kuini's face, spitting tiny remnants of food. "And you cannot interfere. You can just go away, back to your Acolhua losers. Find yourself another emperor."

Kuini could not feel his hands anymore, so tightly were they gripping the carved handle of his sword. The wave was threatening to take him, still he fought it, searching for something to say, not to this lowlife who was trying to pick a fight, but to the two fighting men. He had to stop it. He had to prevent them from killing each other.

He pushed the pressing man aside. "Wait!" he yelled, leaping toward the fighters, oblivious of their swishing weapons.

They paid him no attention, striking and parrying, furious, determined to kill, both of them. Oh, but he knew Coyotl too well. His friend was a reasonable man, but he was a warrior, a veteran of two summers of the Tepanec campaign. The wrathful man of that Iso-girl had underestimated the Lowlander, taking him for a youth, but Coyotl was an experienced warrior, in spite of his age. And so was he, Kuini. And yet, this time the fighting wouldn't do. This time he had to control his temper. If Coyotl managed to kill this man, he would be done for. He was a dead man either way now.

The man with the scar grabbed his upper arm, making him sway. Kuini paid him enough attention to make sure his club was not put to use before pushing his attacker with a ferocious suddenness, putting all of his weight into this unexpected thrust. The man lost his balance and crashed heavily into the dust.

Ducking an onslaught of the third warrior who had kept silent until now, Kuini once again leaped toward the fighting rivals.

"Stop it," he yelled, shoving himself between them, somehow

managing not to get hit by either of the pounding weapons.

They froze for a heartbeat, staring at him, wide-eyed.

"Listen!" Breathing heavily, he straightened up, trying to catch the momentum before they pounced on each other anew. "Don't fight it. Not now. You can do it later. Or bring the matter before the clans' council. Don't fight it here like two outlaws."

"I'm not waiting for your council," growled Iso's man, beads of sweat covering his forehead. "I will kill him now. The cowardly Lowlander will not get a chance to wriggle out by lying to the council."

"I'm not, not do this. No try get away!" cried out Coyotl, eyes flashing. "You cowardly, bring three men to kill, not do this yourself."

"Oh, you are done for!" The older man pounced once again, his club high.

"Wait!" Oblivious of danger, Kuini grabbed the man's arm, stopping the swing of the club in midair with a strength he had not suspected himself capable of. "Do it properly. Through the council. We are not savages; we have laws."

The man's eyes were very close now, gleaming eerily. "I will do my own dirty work, wild boy. I don't need your town's council, the council dominated by your father, another foreigner and lover of Lowlanders."

Kuini felt it like a fist smashing into his stomach. For a moment he could not draw a breath, feeling his insides shrinking, collapsing into each other. Staring into the wide glistening face, seeing every cavity, every bead of sweat, he knew he would have to kill this man whatever the cost. That is, if Coyotl did not finish him first.

Releasing his grip, he took a step back, aware of his surroundings with an unusual clearness. The swish of the club came as no surprise, and he felt his body leaping aside as if watching it from above. A vicious spike sliced the air beside his ear and his sword came to life, moving in an arch, accumulating power, using its own drive. It cut under the man's ribs neatly, accurately, making it look like an easy work.

The face with the scar contorted, shook. The thinly pressed lips opened, letting out a groan, then slipping out of Kuini's sight. The carved handle of his sword slid, and he fought not to let it go, panicking now that the man was taking his weapon down with him. It was stuck deeply in the mess of the broken ribs, and the twists of the wounded body made it impossible for Kuini to get a better grip.

More people surrounded them now. He could sense their presence, could hear their agitated voices. Clenching his teeth, he pulled frantically, listening to the screams of the man on the ground. *Who were those people? More enemies?*

A familiar hiss brought him back to reality. He threw himself aside, and the blow, that could have broken his back, brushed against his shoulder, sending him sprawling over the squirming man he had just cut. Rolling over, he tried again to reach for his sword, but instead his hands grabbed the smooth handle of his fallen enemy's club.

The second man attacked anew, and Kuini had hardly enough time to scramble to his feet, his club blocking the blow, but badly. Only half upright, he was in no position to hold out against the pressure.

In a desperate attempt to catch his balance, he pounced aside, the club slippery in his sweaty palms. Long summers fighting with a sword had made him forget how to use a club. Luckily, his opponent took his time, planning his next onslaught carefully. It gave Kuini a heartbeat to stabilize himself while also shooting a quick glance around.

A small crowd surrounded them now, watching intently, their disapproval open. From the corner of his eye, he could see Coyotl and his rival, still fighting, both bloodied and gasping, but as fierce and as determined as before.

Shifting his grip upon his club, Kuini met the new attack more readily, forcing himself to remember that no sharp spikes adorned the edges of his new weapon. He would have to direct his blows differently, not trying to cut but to smash.

The man on the ground stopped screaming, unconscious or already dead, and Kuini pressed forward, trying to direct their retreat toward the bloody mess. He just needed to get his sword back!

He heard people gasping but did not dare to take his eyes off the threatening club, fighting the temptation to do so. They did nothing outstanding, so the crowd must have been reacting to the other fight.

His attention now only partly on what he was doing, Kuini blocked the next blow, his senses probing, feeling the mounting agitation of the people around them. He could see the hesitation in his opponent's eyes. They stared at each other for another heartbeat and then, at the imperceptible nod of the other man, Kuini let his glance wander toward the surrounding people and then the edge of the clearing.

His heart stopped, then threw itself wildly against his ribs. Coyotl, disheveled and smeared with blood, some of which was obviously his, stood above his fallen enemy, legs wide apart. His torn cloak swaying rhythmically, hands clutching the rising and falling sword, he hacked at the motionless body again and again, making a bloody mess out of what used to be an imposing man, a prominent warrior and a renowned hunter. Pieces of flesh and broken obsidian splattered all around, and Coyotl's face looked wild and unrecognizable, distorted with so much insanely professed rage that Kuini winced. As if in a dream, he watched his friend butchering the already dead enemy as though afraid he might spring back to life if he stopped.

The memory of the Texcoco Palace surfaced, making his stomach heave. Three summers had passed, and he had become an experienced warrior, yet the picture of the dismembered body of a man who had tried to kill the Aztec Warlord would always do this to him. A youth of only fifteen back then, it was the first time he had seen what an obsidian sword could do. This was also the first time he had come to discover that even a very brave warrior could lose control of his senses, succumbing to the pure fury, and maybe even a surge of panic, taking it all out on the already killed enemy.

As if sensing the shock of the onlookers, Coyotl's hands shook and did not raise again. Taking a convulsive breath, the Lowlander stood there for a moment, his back still to the crowds.

Then, wiping his face with the back of his hand, smearing fresh blood upon it, he turned around, returning people's gazes, eyes dark and still wild, still challenging, but changing rapidly.

Blinking, Kuini watched the sanity flowing back into the well familiar face, smoothing its features. His stomach twisted, and he took a step forward, unable to stand the desperation in his friend's eyes. Always reserved, always pleasant, Coyotl rarely shared his real feelings, concealing his frustration well, even from his best friend, but it was out there now for everyone to see.

Oblivious of his previous rival and the people all around them, Kuini crossed the clearing, careful not to slip on the wet rocks, now glittering with too much crimson. He felt his friend tensing as his eyes met the anguished gaze, saw the dark enlarged pupils.

"It's all good," he said, putting his arm over Coyotl's shoulder. "It's over."

The tensed muscles relaxed at once under his touch. The wide shoulders sagged, then straightened up.

"It sort of went out of hand, didn't it?" muttered Coyotl, forcing a smile.

"Oh, yes, but it was a sight worth seeing."

A reluctant grin. "So, what now?"

They looked up, meeting the frozen stares of the silent crowd, seeing the stony faces, the tightened lips, the open disgust in the narrowed pairs of eyes. The hostility was so tangible one seemed to be able to touch it through the thick air.

An elderly man Kuini recognized as a leader of one of the clans parted from the crowd.

"You two, go and wash up, then follow me," he said curtly, nearing them, his paces long, eyes unbearably cold. "Hurry!"

So they were not about to be torn apart by the angry mob, reflected Kuini numbly, suddenly aware of his own strained muscles and taut nerves. He forced himself to relax, knowing that the elderly man would see through him easily. This was not the time to feel angry or resentful, or worst of all, frightened. No. Whatever the decision the heads of the clans arrived at, he would face it with dignity. He would not make his father ashamed, and if it were up to him, he would not let them use it against the formidable man either.

The blood still seeped out of the gash on Coyotl's arm, and the side of the Lowlander's forehead was bloody and horribly swollen. How did he manage to go on fighting after such a blow? wondered Kuini, keeping close as they descended the riverbank, ready to catch his friend should he fall.

The Lowlander's face was stark, grayish and lifeless in the strong high noon sun. Watching the unsteady paces, the desperately clasped mouth, Kuini asked himself if his friend would be allowed to see a healer. Or would they decide it was a waste of time, to treat a man who was destined to die?

CHAPTER 11

Taking the boiling pot off the fire, Mino cursed as her fingers slipped and the drops of hot water splashed all around. She put the pot on the earthen floor, then straightened up and cursed some more.

"Let me help you, Honorable Mother," said Ino, coming behind her quietly. "Let me do this for you."

"You can't make medicine." Sighing, she moderated her tone, aware that the sweet, helpful First Wife of her First Son had nothing to do with any of it. "It's just that the stupid pot almost toppled all over me."

The plump woman returned her gaze, her forehead creased above her sad eyes. "You can instruct me as to what to do, and I'll do it. You are tired and should rest."

Mino forced a smile. "I'm not that old, girl. I can prepare a medicine. It's just..." She brought her hand to her eyes, rubbing them tiredly. "I wish they would come home already."

The round face of her son's wife twisted, turned sadder. "Me too. I wish none of it had happened."

"But it did!" Mino felt like cursing again, her rage sudden and overwhelming.

How could her son have been so stupid? Hadn't he caused enough trouble by bringing his highborn Lowlander here? But now? Oh, now, after what those two had done, the mere presence of the heir to the Texcoco throne here in the Highlands looked like something completely ordinary.

"It's my fault," she said tiredly. "He came to talk to his father yesterday, and I yelled at him and scared him away. I should have been more patient."

Ino's eyes flashed. "It is not your fault, Honorable Mother. It is his fault. Your youngest son is wild, and he is short-tempered, and he keeps a strange company. He has always been a strange boy, and he didn't improve over the summers he has been wandering gods-know-where."

"He is not!" Angrily, Mino busied herself stirring the contents of another pot full of cooked maguey sap. "He is a good boy. He just can't find his purpose in life." She smelled the ointment absently, then picked up a little of it with her finger, feeling it out. "He should not have come back. Wherever he was he felt better there than here. I can tell."

"Then why did he come back?"

"Because of the Lowlander. Why else?"

The pudgy woman pursed her lips. "Like I said, your son keeps a strange company. No wonder it brought him no good." She waved her arms in the air. "They shouldn't have allowed the Lowlander to stay here, your son or not. They should have killed him right away, sacrificed him in the temple of our mighty *Camaxtli*. As it is, they waited until the lowly man went and killed a good warrior. What good did it do? Oh, I hope they'll sacrifice him now."

Mino sighed, knowing that the silly woman was right, even if partly.

"You are talking nonsense, Ino. Mighty *Camaxtli* deserves the hearts and the life forces of captured warriors. This particular Lowlander could not be sacrificed unless captured in battle." She shrugged. "And even if you would want to count his inglorious hand-to-hand of this morning, which is absolutely inappropriate, you can't even do that, because he did not lose that combat either. He killed his rival in a fair hand-to-hand."

Scowling, the plump woman busied herself sorting pottery bowls. "My husband is furious since this afternoon. He knew Yoho well, you know. They fought together once and hunted many times." Atypically upset, she took a convulsive breath. "I can't believe this great hunter and warrior was killed by the filthy, cowardly Lowlander, and in our own homeland."

"We don't know what happened, what truly happened there." Absently, Mino picked a pile of *chili* leaves and began grinding them in a deep bowl.

"We do know what happened. Plenty of people saw it. The filthy Lowlander took Yoho's wife, then he went and killed that great hunter and warrior."

As the grinding stone smashed against her finger, Mino stifled a curse once again. "That warrior was not such a great person," she said finally. "He was a cruel, self-centered, bad-tempered man. He was afraid of Nihi, so he would behave when in his house, but he was not always that way. I saw him behaving disgustingly to people sometimes."

"But the Lowlander lay with his wife!" cried Ino hotly. "Every man would behave disgustingly over something like that."

"Of course. I'm not defending the Lowlander. I'm just trying to say that it may not have been the way you heard it was." She studied the contents of the bowl, running her fingers through the powder she'd created. No need to concentrate while doing this; she had been making medicine for longer than she could remember. "This boy was always so nice, so well-behaved. I didn't like him finding shelter in our lands anymore than you did, but only because of his origins. For himself, he seemed like a nice boy." Her stomach tightened at the thought of her son. "I hope they will find a solution."

"For your son they will," said Ino, her placid, sweet-natured self again. "I'm sure of that and it will be good." A soft palm rested upon Mino's arm, warm and reassuring. "I'll make offering for him to calm down and begin living a good life."

As a shadow fell across the doorway they raised their heads, watching Nihi squeezing himself through the gaping entrance, his usually pleasantly serious face grim, eyes dark and stormy. Not sparing the two women a glance, he nodded a curt greeting, then went toward the fire, sinking heavily onto one of the mats, his shoulders sagging.

"Here, take it." Eyeing the crunchy powder in her bowl, Mino scowled, forcing her thoughts to concentrate, her heart beating fast. To pour the ground leaves into the larger vessel containing the cooked sap proved a challenging business. "You keep stirring it and don't stop. We need it smooth and well mixed."

Not checking with the younger woman to see if her instructions were understood or followed, she turned around and headed toward the squatting figure of her oldest son.

He squatted there, staring into the fire, breathing heavily, his formidable fists clenched, eyes blazing. Oh, but she had rarely seen him that angry, a man of well over thirty summers, greatly appreciated and content with his life, a future leader beyond any doubt. Finding it difficult to utter the question, she sat beside him, watching the fire.

"I could kill this useless piece of meat," growled Nihi eventually. "This good for nothing brother of mine."

She swallowed. "How is it going out there?"

"How do you think it is going, Mother?" he asked through his clenched teeth.

She clasped her palms tight. "Badly for your father."

"Of course!" She could feel him tensing, clenching his fists anew. "He is doing his best to keep his presence of mind. I don't know how he is doing it, with Ai, this dirty piece of rotten meat, accusing him now openly of all sort of things, from defending the two stupid hotheads, to betraying our people by suggesting we fight with the Lowlanders for a change. Filthy, stinking piece of excrement!" His voice rose, then shook. "And it's not that he is coveting Father's position. He is too old, too cowardly, too useless to try and lead our people instead of Father. Oh, no! All he wants is to see Father out of the council house. He's envied Father for summers, but now, thanks to that stupid brother of mine, he has a perfect opportunity to spill his venom."

Her stomach shrank and she could not get enough air.

"But others," she said helplessly. "They love your father. They trusted him for countless summers to lead and to advice. Surely they wouldn't listen to a malicious rat bursting with jealousy at the abilities of another man."

"Oh, had it happened a summer or two ago, before the Acolhua scum lost their lands, before the Tepanecs, before our precious Kuini brought the Lowlander here, yes, they would listen to him and they would not question his decisions. But now?" The wide shoulders lifted in a shrug. "Now they are not so certain they can trust Father's judgment. He is adamant about the danger of the Tepanecs. And his origins, his connections in the Aztec capital are doubtful, to say the least."

"Oh, don't start it you too!" cried Mino hotly. "His origins are immaterial. He is a perfect highlander, and he was good enough to lead our people for summers. They should go on trusting his judgment. He is wise and he is brave, and he has a better grasp on history and the happenings in the whole region than all of them put together."

She glared at her son, furious and somehow glad to take her penned up frustration out on something in particular. Or someone. The thought made her uncomfortable and she moderated her tone.

"Maybe it's because he was brought up on the other side of the Great Lake actually, you know? His knowledge is broader because of his origins, and people should use it instead of mistrusting it. He is like an eagle, flying so high he can see the land spread before him, while his eyes are sharp enough to see the whole picture and the small details in it."

"Well, maybe it's time he came closer to the ground," said Nihi gloomily, shrugging again. "There are small details he is obviously missing. Like the enmity of some people nurtured over the summers. Like the reluctance of others to accept his far-fetched ideas. Like the inability of his own youngest son to do one reasonable thing in his whole stupid, worthless life." He took a deep breath and the air hissed, having difficulty breaking through his clenched teeth. "He keeps defending him, keeps trying to see the sense in what the stupid hothead is doing. But there is no sense in Kuini's actions. He is just a spoiled brat who is trying to feel special by doing different things; and he doesn't care if it brings trouble to other people." The dark eyes flashed. "Father should stop trying to help him out, should let him solve his own problems, with Lowlanders and with himself!"

Sighing, Mino stared at the fire, knowing that Nihi was right. Of course he was! And yet, her youngest son was not selfish and not spoiled. He was not the type to try and gain attention by acting wildly. He had never been this way, not even when small, the last of her children, so much younger than his brothers, and therefore, always apart and somewhat overlooked. Usually quiet and reserved, Kuini had kept his own counsel, rarely sharing his thoughts or adventures, spending his time outside, doing gods-know-what. She had been too busy to pay attention; he had been the easiest of her sons.

She stared at the fire, remembering Kuini as a boy, tall and slender, and unafraid, always unafraid, watching the world thoughtfully, with those keen Tepanec eyes of his. Was his father right about him? Was he deeper than they all thought? Could he have seen something they had missed, with their gazes clouded by prejudice? He was so much like his father in some ways.

"I don't know," she said tiredly. "Maybe we should trust your father's opinions more. Maybe he sees something we don't."

"Or maybe he is just trying to help, like any father would." Nihi grunted and shifted his eyes back to the fire. "I know how it is. I have sons of my own. But I'll keep a close eye on them, so none of them will turn out to be as messed up as Kuini." Another grunt. "He should have stayed in the Lowlands. This way we would never have known where he was spending his time, and we would just miss him and remember him for the best."

The pain in her chest grew. Blinking away the suspicious wetness that was threatening to blur her vision, Mino watched her son's wife coming toward them, carrying the bowl.

"I think the ointment is ready, Honorable Mother," said the plump woman quietly, shooting a worried glance toward her husband. "Should I take it to the council house now?"

"No. We will wait for them to come here." Mino rose to her feet with difficulty. "I suppose their wounds are not that bad if they didn't send for the medicine yet."

Coyotl blinked, trying to banish the grayish mist that kept

gathering in the corners of his eyes. It would come, flickering prettily with each new wave of nausea, making him wish to shut his eyes. A luxury that he could not afford. Not in the room full of impatient, arguing people, most of whom kept shooting furious glances in his direction. And, anyway, when he tried to shut his eyes for a heartbeat, when no one seemed to look, it only made his nausea worse, so every time it happened, he would take a deep breath and wait for the new wave to recede.

"Then you are saying the crimes that those two have committed should be overlooked, go unpunished?" The slight sinewy man almost yelled now, making Coyotl's headache worse. "What have we come to, I'm asking you? Are we savages with no laws, people who are sorting out their differences by simply killing each other? Do we have no clans, no councils? Are our leaders that worthless?" The squinted eyes narrowed, blazing with fire. "Or did we turn into a lawless society since the Tepanecs took the Lowlands, forcing Acolhua refugees on us, making our leaders nervous and unsure of themselves."

Understanding the general gist, Coyotl turned to watch Kuini's father, yet the sharp movement sent a shaft of agonizing pain rolling from his swollen forehead all the way down his spine, taking his breath away. His vision blurred, and it took him more than a few heartbeats before he was able to listen again.

"No one is suggesting to allow the crime go unpunished. Our laws are wise and provide for many such problems to be solved." The War Leader's voice was low but still calm, still in control, although he had been arguing with many people by now, getting accused almost openly by some, mostly by that sinewy angry man.

Mesmerized, Coyotl watched the narrow face, set and looking as if chiseled out of stone, seeing the clenched jaw, the dark eyes. He remembered talking to this man only this morning, the way he had come in afraid and went out elated, admiring the old leader's wisdom and grasp, becoming fond of the light twinkle flickering in the depths of the prominent eyes. It was all set this morning, his future and a new purpose in life. But now, only half a day later, it was all lost, lost to his own recklessness, and his stupidity, and his inability to control himself, whether in taking women who belonged to other men or in facing their enraged husbands with presence of mind. And worst of all, he had let people who were helping him down, dragging them into his trouble along with him, Kuini and his father.

He glanced at his friend who had squatted beside him, motionless like a stone statue. The Highlander had still been unafraid, still in high spirits, when they had gone down to wash the blood and the dust off, supporting Coyotl, checking on his wounds, talking as if it was another of their crazy adventures on the Tepanec side of the Great Lake, or even back in the Texcoco Palace where the reckless hothead had gotten himself into a whole bunch of trouble three summers ago. Yet now, in the cramped council house, watching his father being attacked, accused of all sorts of crimes and underlying motives, Kuini had lost the remnants of his cheeky brazenness, freezing as if turned into a stone, with only his eyes blazing and alive, listening intently, leaping from face to face.

Coyotl's heard squeezed, for he knew what effort it cost his friend to hang onto his temper, to listen impartially and in silence, knowing it was mostly his fault. Clenching his teeth, he concentrated on the forceful voice of the War Leader.

"I do say that the council of the clans should be called in order to discuss these youths' crimes. Only the leaders of the clans, gathered together, should be allowed to determine the nature of the punishment, according to whether the murder was warranted or not, whether the offending side was actually defending itself as some of the witnesses testified."

"The offending side took his victim's wife and then proceeded to kill the man," cried out Ai. By now Coyotl had learned the sinewy man's name. "The insolent Lowlander did not try to deny any of that. What is the nature of the inquiries that you wish the leaders of the clans to make? Or is it just an attempt to gain time, to try to sway people to your side?"

The War Leader's eyes blazed murder. "What are you accusing me of?" he growled, suddenly menacing and dangerous. Despite the unimpressive height and the lean disposition, the man radiated much power, doubled now that his temper seemed to snap. "If someone has been going around, spreading gossip, talking about one's rivals behind their backs, it is not me but you! So you had better not push it in this direction."

The light in the low building seemed to dim, and busy fighting his blinding headache, Coyotl could hear people shifting uneasily.

"I do see the merit in calling the council of the clans," said a tall man with matted hair and a dirty, reeking cloak, clearly a priest. "If for no other reason than because it was not a murder, but a willing duel, agreed upon between both sides." The man shrugged. "Even if this crime was committed by a foreigner and for despicable reasons."

"Not just a foreigner but a sworn enemy of our people," exclaimed Ai, seemingly unimpressed by the War Leader's previous outburst. "Our glorious Warriors' Leader keeps forgetting this little piece of information."

But Kuini's father seemed to have regained his previous composure. "This youth is not a sworn enemy of our people, whatever his origins. Given his age, if not his intentions, he has never fought against our people. By the time he'd become a warrior, his people were engaged in their war against the Tepanecs—"

"With one particular Highlander in the lead of those ill-fated raids!" Ai cut into the man's speech, his voice trembling with rage.

The air hissed loudly, escaping the War Leader's clenched teeth, but still he managed to hold onto his temper.

"I doubt that a youth of my son's age was allowed to lead any forces of warriors," he said, his eyes narrow, lips twisting with open disdain. "The Lowlanders are not that useless. But then, what would you know about any of that? You've never led warriors. Or any other people. I can understand your ignorance."

The other man's face twisted, but he also managed to control himself. "I trust you to know all about the Lowlanders and their uselessness or usefulness. Given your origins and upbringing, you should know."

The air in the room thickened. "Yes, I know many useful things. My opinions are thoughtful, well informed, and worth listening to." The War Leader's voice was just a little more strained, but Coyotl saw the tight jaw and the darker shade that spread across the man's sharp cheekbones.

The thickset man squatting beside the fire did not rise to his feet, yet when he spoke the heads turned as if pushed in the direction of the calm voice.

"Then it boils down to the question of whether to hand the foreigner over to the family of the killed man or to summon the heads of the clans in order to ask for their collective advice." The penetrating eyes encircled those present in the room, lingering upon the two enraged opponents. "We gathered here this afternoon to discuss this matter and this matter alone. Any other debate should be left for another time and another place. Or better yet, solved privately and with dignity and self respect." His gaze lingered on the sinewy man's face for only a fraction of a moment longer, but it was enough to make its recipient blush. "Now, I wish to hear our War Leader out. Why do you think this particular Lowlander should be treated differently?"

For the first time, Coyotl saw Kuini's father licking his lips, narrowing his eyes, his high forehead creasing.

"As I said before," he began slowly, "we should understand that the Acolhua Lowlanders are of no consequence to us, not anymore. They do not exist, not as a power. So this youth's origins are immaterial now. Yet, his spirit, his personality matter. This heir to the Texcoco throne is nothing but a youth, the youth who formed friendships with Highlanders while still a noble Acolhua, the youth who came here willingly, the youth who has lived here for seasons, learning our ways. One day, he may get his *altepetl* and his provinces back, and then, he might be of a great use to us. Supported by Texcoco, Huexotzinco could prosper like it never has before. Opening our minds just a little, opening our thoughts to logic and reason, we could help it happen instead of killing it before it could blossom and bear a fruit. Why let the old prejudice cloud our vision? Because it's easy and comfortable?" A fleeting grin stretched the thin lips, and the man's gaze traveled from face to face, now calm and forceful, remaining Coyotl of the morning conversation. "We all know that the easiest way is not always the better one. Sometimes people, or nations, are required to take more difficult, less familiar paths. But if those bring us to a better future, why would we try to spare ourselves an effort?"

Forgetting his headache and his nausea, Coyotl listened, mesmerized, knowing that this speech must have been more beautiful, more logical, if fully understood. He felt more than saw Kuini leaning forward, afraid to miss a word. The room went so quiet he could hear a buzzing of the insects beside the flickering torch.

"I love what you have said, Leader of the Warriors," said the thickset man, getting to his feet. "I always trusted your judgment and your common sense. But for the incident we came to discuss tonight, I may have asked you to expand on your vision, your idea of using this particular Lowlander."

The man paused, pursed his lips as if deliberating. No one said a word, no one tried to interrupt. *Must be someone of great importance,* reflected Coyotl numbly.

"Alas, what happened today cannot go unnoticed, or unattended. The family of the dead man will demand justice. Rightfully so. I agree that the leaders of all our clans should be allowed to speak their minds. I agree we cannot just hand this foreigner to the mourning relatives of the victim's family. But I don't believe this youth will have the chance of participating in bringing our War Leader's vision of peace to life." He shrugged, glancing at Kuini's father with what seemed like a genuine regret. "Maybe someone else will do it one day, oh very wise and open-minded Leader of the Warriors. Who knows? Gods are acting strange in the best of times and people should accept their interference with dignity and a certain amount of humbleness. We should not try to influence the events more than necessary." The gaze bore into the War Leader, suddenly heavy with meaning. "Do you agree with me, Old Friend?"

Kuini's father returned the gaze, seemingly calm, but his jaw was clenched and his nostrils widened with every breath.

"Of course I agree, Honorable Leader," he said in a steady voice. "Any other way of behavior would not be wise, would it?"

"No, it would not." The man looked around the room again.

"As your son is involved in this and the foreigner was housed in your family, I'm asking you to give the accused a shelter until the council will meet to decide this youth's fate." The gaze hardened once again, turned piercing, penetrating. "Both youths will be your responsibility until the decision will be reached."

He sensed the stone statue of his friend coming back to life, letting out a held breath. Busy fighting the new wave of nausea, gathering all his strength for the effort of getting up, he bit his lips, suddenly afraid he wouldn't be able to make his way to the War Leader's house. It was so horribly far, and every careless movement made his head spin with pain, with even a slight draft brushing against his forehead forcing him to clench his teeth in agony.

And yet, he knew that he would make his way proudly and with every bit of dignity he could muster. The War Leader believed in him; he had said so in front of all those people.

CHAPTER 12

"This swelling is bad and has to be opened."

Lingering at respectable distance, Kuini watched his mother standing on her tiptoes in order to study Coyotl's forehead. Careful not to touch the wound, she reached out, pushing some of the sweaty hair away, making the tall Acolhua sway, gasping with pain.

Involuntarily, Kuini moved closer, ready to catch his friend should he start falling, eyeing the grayish, lifeless face, the clouded eyes, the painfully pressed lips, wondering how the Lowlander had made his way here at all.

"Sit here," said the mistress of the house, her bright yellow eyes unreadable. "Or better still, lay over there." She pointed at the pile of mats near the fire, turning to Kuini. "Take him there and make him lie down."

For a heartbeat, Kuini just stared, trying to comprehend the fact that now his mother, the priestess of the Obsidian Butterfly Goddess, was speaking to him in the Lowlanders' Nahuatl.

"Well?"

He shook off the strange sensation. *Another thing to wonder about later on.* Taking most of Coyotl's weight, he led his friend toward the indicated spot.

"You'll be fine," he said quietly, sensing his friend's exhaustion; and his fear. "Mother is good with healing. She'll help."

In the meantime, a plump woman Kuini recognized as his eldest brother's First Wife brought a bowl of a strange smelling brew.

"Keep stirring it," said his mother, addressing the woman briskly, in command as always. Her gaze came to rest on Kuini once again, businesslike, impartial. "Take your knife and hold it over the fire. Count to twenty, then turn it around and do the same to the other side."

Kuini blinked. "I will."

The heat scorched his palms, but he held the knife over the raging fire, beneath another pot full of boiling water. He counted slowly. Half twenty, then twenty, then another half. Turning the knife over, he held his breath, trying to listen to the muffled voices coming from the patio where Father and Nihi had been arguing since they had all come here.

His stomach shrank once again at the thought of his father. He *needed* to talk to the man. Yet, what was there to talk about now? What could he say? And surely not with Nihi there, shooting those dark glares full of so much loathing and disdain Kuini felt like smashing something. He knew he was a lowlife beyond any contempt, a dirty piece of excrement that had ruined their father. He knew it too well all by himself.

"You don't have to melt this thing." Mother's voice broke into his thoughts, and he winced, suddenly aware of the pain in his palms, the carved hilt of the knife cutting into his skin, nicking it from the force with which he held it. "Come here and hold your friend so he won't move."

He handed her the knife reluctantly, moving his fingers to return the feeling into his numb, hurting palms. He knew he should say something, but his teeth were clenched so tight he thought he would never be able to unclench them.

"Here, take this." Leaning closer to Coyotl, who watched her with a painfully concentrated gaze, she nodded, once again talking in her accented but clear Nahuatl.

Where did she learn to speak this tongue? wondered Kuini randomly, glad to take his thoughts off what was transpiring. He watched his friend's eyes filling with fear as a small piece of lined wood was tucked into his mouth.

"You just fasten your teeth around it," went on Mother, a little more kindly. "It'll hurt but only for a little while." She turned to

Kuini. "You sit here and hold him by whatever means. I need him perfectly still." Shifting her grip on the knife, holding it with the expertise of a priestess, she glanced at Nihi's wife. "You, be ready with the cloths. Just wet them one after another and give them to me. And throw the dirty pile into the boiling pot."

Forgetting his own troubled thoughts, Kuini crouched beside his friend.

"It's all going to be well," he whispered, taking hold of the wide shoulders, pressing against the Lowlander's leaner frame, ready to use his whole weight to prevent it from moving. "It'll be over in a heartbeat. She'll make it neat and quick, you'll see. She is a great healer."

The wild, frightened gaze held his, but he saw Coyotl's head nodding slightly, imperceptibly.

"It's going to be well, truly." Helplessly, he hardly noticed he was still talking, seeing the colorless lips moving, adjusting around the wooden piece. The panicked gaze left Kuini's face, following the knife.

"Hold him!"

Her hand took a firmer hold of the Lowlander's swollen forehead, and Kuini could hear the gritting of the wooden piece when Coyotl's teeth fastened around it. Putting all his weight against the arching body, he held his breath as the knife came down, cutting the swollen flesh swiftly, determinedly. It took all of his strength, or what was left of it, to prevent the jerking limbs from escaping his grip.

Clenching his teeth, he almost shut his eyes, listening to the strangled, bubbling screams ringing beside his ear. *Oh gods, let it be over soon*, he thought, holding on with the last of his strength. *Why does she hurt him this way?*

The body underneath went limp so suddenly, he almost slipped over it as Coyotl's strained face lost all traces of life and his eyes rolled, still wide open but now lacking the enlarged pupils, displaying the frightening whiteness instead.

"Move." His mother's calm voice penetrated the fog in his mind.

Pushing Kuini away, she leaned forward, listening to Coyotl's heartbeat. *Was he still alive?*

Apparently satisfied with what her senses related to her, she nodded and went back wiping the bloody mess off Coyotl's forehead, pressing it expertly, making the foul-smelling yellowish liquid trickle out, snatching clean cloths from Nihi's wife's lifeless hands.

Kuini's gaze brushed past the pasty face of the frightened woman, then came back to what his mother was doing, fascinated.

"This is what caused all the pain," he heard her murmuring, as if talking to herself. "Amazing how a small cut can make such a great difference."

"Will he feel better when he comes back to life?" asked Kuini, aware of his own strained muscles relaxing.

"Oh, yes. I think he'll feel much better. Unless the blow did more damage than I think." She shrugged, taking another wet cloth. "I think the club only brushed against his head, which is lucky. Better directed, it would have cracked his skull."

Surprised, Kuini shifted his gaze to her absorbed face, then followed her briskly moving hands. "You know much about warfare."

"I'm old enough to learn a thing or two, don't you think?" There was a grin to her voice now. "Living with a leading warrior helps a woman to come to all sorts of information." She glanced up, her eyes bright, twinkling with a hint of mischief. "We are not helpless creatures some of you take us for."

He grinned against his will. "I never made this mistake. Growing up in this particular household, how could I?"

Her smile widened. "Well, now Ino, take all this filth and throw it into the boiling pot." She leaned forward, inspecting her work. "I should have sewn this cut, but I want to leave it open, to let it drain some more." Shrugging, she straightened up. "He'll sport a neat little scar to remember this incident. Bring me the bowl with the ointment."

The thick mash smelled fresh and spicy, not like her usual brews. "Thank you, Mother," he said, coming back, carrying the vessel. He watched her small, wrinkled palms moving briskly, smearing the ointment over the now-clean cut. "I wish I could repay you your kindness. All of you."

She looked up fleetingly, her strange eyes not yellow but honey colored now, kind and soft, radiating warm reassurance.

"You will be fine," she said quietly, a smile transforming her face, making it look younger. "I used to argue with your father, but now I think he was right about you. You will make us all proud yet."

His throat tightened. "No, I won't," he said, swallowing hard. "I keep messing up everything I do." He took a deep breath, clenching his teeth to make his voice stop trembling. "I'll be outside. Call me if you need me."

The freshness of the night enveloped him, welcoming in its quiet tranquility. He perched on the stump of an old tree, remembering this favorite spot of his since being a child. Protected from being seen from the house by the thick bushes, it offered a good view of the muddy road beyond his mother's rows of plants.

Clasping his palms together, he watched the dark sky, seeing none of its beauty. The memories of the cramped council house flooded in, mercilessly vivid. He remembered his father's face, set and stony, with the usually grinning mouth clasped tight and the prominent eyes dark and blazing. How had it come to this? How had this formidable man, this great leader of many summers, come to be accused of every crime possible? Where had all the venom, all the hidden envy come from?

He suppressed a groan, knowing the answer to that. Leadership inspired jealousy, and there were always people, petty, shabby, uninspiring types, who would use every excuse to bring a great man down. Oh, yes, there was nothing new about that. He had spent enough time among the highest circles of the Lowlanders to learn this simple fact of life. Great men lived with that, and his father, oh such a wise, perceptive, experienced leader, knew all about it, of that Kuini was sure. Yet, even such a great man must have been surprised. No one expects to come down because of one's son.

He shut his eyes against the pain. The taste of blood on his tongue was salty, but he welcomed it. He wished he could offer all his blood to make things right again. Maybe on the altar of mighty *Camaxtli*, or the Lowlanders' *Tezcatlipoca*. He would let them cut his chest gladly for the chance to undo everything he had done.

Seeing the familiar lean silhouette heading up the path, stepping over the low bushes, he shrunk deeper into the shadows, his heart beating fast. Straining his eyes, he tried to see through the darkness, to decipher what the familiar face held, willing the man to turn toward the house, wishing him to make his way toward his hidden place.

As if sensing the ardent scrutiny, the man slowed his paces, his warrior's instincts clearly telling him he was being watched. Another heartbeat of hesitation, and he turned toward the bushes concealing Kuini's semi-hidden spot.

"Father!'

In the moonlight he saw the creases lining the high forehead smoothing, the familiar lips stretching into an amused grin.

"You better come in," called out the War Leader lightly, still distant, still not intimate. "I'm sure you can use some sleep given your recent activities."

Kuini hesitated, raising to his feet hastily, searching for something to say. He needed to start somewhere, but what could one say to a man who had given one his life and everything, getting back nothing but an offensive anger and unreasonable expectations.

He watched Father's face changing, losing its distant expression.

"Come on in," said the man more softly, resuming his walk toward the house.

Kuini took a deep breath. "Father, wait. I... I need to talk to you."

The man didn't slow his step. "No, you don't. Talk to me when you are ready, not a heartbeat before."

He felt the darkness closing on him, the air around him suddenly empty, lacking its vital qualities. It made him dizzy.

"Father, please." He fought the urge to grab the man's arm, to physically stop him from leaving, suddenly longing to talk, to have this great man all for himself, even for a short while. "Please.

I'm not trying to talk to you because of what happened. I came here on the evening before. I was ready then. I wanted to talk to you, but you were busy and then, then something happened, and I could not come back." He drew another deep breath. "I did not want any of it to happen. I wish I could do something, anything, to prevent any of it. And I'm sorry for everything. For bringing Coyotl here, but also for going away without telling you. And for being angry with you about things that you should not have to apologize for." He clenched his teeth to stop his voice from trembling. "I know it is not something you can just forget or forgive. But I want you to know that I'm sorry about it all and that I will do anything I can to make it right again."

His whole being concentrated on the effort to control his voice, he winced as the rough palm rested upon his shoulder.

"Come," said the man, and there was no trace of the previous lightness or amusement in the low voice. "You are most certainly ready, and your timing could not be better." The heavy arm propelled him back toward the muddy road.

Afraid to let the hope enter his mind, Kuini followed, his heart beating fast. *Where were they going?* The night enveloped them, soundless and tranquil, with their quiet warriors' steps not breaking the silence but adding to it.

"We don't have enough time to head out for the woods," said the War Leader finally, slowing his paces when no stone houses surrounded them. "But this limited amount of privacy will do."

Kuini felt the thoughtful eyes turning to him, measuring him calmly, unhurriedly. He straightened his gaze. "Why did we have to leave the house in order to talk?"

The dark eyes flickered with amusement. "Because we need to discuss things privately."

"Oh!"

"Yes, oh. And we do not have much time, either." Frowning, the man shrugged. "Although, your friend's condition may prove difficult to deal with."

"Mother said he'll be well again."

"Yes, but how fast? You'll need him fully capable and not swaying, colorless, and hardly alive." Another shrug. "A fascinating young man, I must say. We had an interesting conversation only this morning."

Kuini halted abruptly. "You talked to Coyotl? Why?"

"Well, he came looking for you, thinking you would be in my house." Father's voice shook with amusement. "Does your friend know you so little?" The grin widened. "And then we talked, politics and history mainly. He is an interesting boy with most unusual ideas."

"Coyotl would make a good emperor, Father. He is very smart, and he is open-minded. He has patience, he listens to people, and he can lead too, while being a good warrior already."

"Oh yes, he can fight. He proved it this afternoon. It was quite a sight, so I was told."

"Well, yes it was, but..." Kuini hesitated. "Father, the things they said in the council house today were lies. He didn't seek to kill this man. Yes, he lay with his woman, but he didn't know she belonged to a man, you see. He didn't know this. And when we were attacked, I tried to stop it. I tried to make them bring the matter to the council house, you see? But of course, they just wanted to kill him and be done with it." A shrug proved a difficult business. "So we had to fight. But it's not like we were looking for it. Coyotl is not like that. He was grateful to the Huexotzinco people for giving him shelter. He liked his life here. He never sought to harm anyone." He took a deep breath. "I was the problem. As always. I almost killed that youth last night, but there was this girl. She stopped the fight and then she told me, she told me about those people trying to reach you through me, because I'm such a hothead with no restraint. So I did my best to stop that fight when they attacked Coyotl. Still, it didn't work and those people managed to get you through me." He stopped, short of breath once again, peering into the darkness before his eyes.

"What girl? What did she say?" He felt more than saw his father turning sharply.

The night lost its tranquility once again. "She was just a girl, and, well, she happened to overhear people talking about it, influential people."

"Who?"

"She didn't know any of them, but according to her description Ai was there, doing most of the talking. He nearly caught her, too."

"Who else?" It came out sharply, an order from the Warriors' Leader.

"She didn't know." Kuini shifted uneasily. "I was on my way to tell you that when I ran into Coyotl and his trouble." The night's sounds were back, interrupting the heavy silence. "I should have come right away."

"Why didn't you?"

"I…"

He could hear his father chuckling in the darkness, not a merry sound but still a chuckle. "If the girl went to all this trouble for you, I suppose she deserved some of your time."

He felt his cheeks warming and was grateful for the cover of the darkness. "I should have come right away!"

"It wouldn't have changed a thing." Paces long and steady, his father resumed their walk. "This or that benevolent spirit gave Ai a much better chance before the filthy piece of dung could be forced into provoking you." The man shook his head. "Well, what's done is done, and there is no point in regretting anything. In the meanwhile, you two will have to prepare to leave. Preferably tonight, although I'm not certain it will be possible with the Lowlander's cracked head."

Once again, Kuini stopped dead in his tracks.

"Father, we cannot leave! The head of the town's council made you responsible for us. He said so in front of all people. He made himself perfectly clear." He peered at the narrowing eyes, trying to see what they held. "We are not going anywhere, Father."

The wide palm came to rest on his shoulder. "Of course, you are going. But you are not running away. You will start working, working hard to implement my plans. You will work for the future of the Lowlands and the Highlands alike, Kuini. I'm not trying to help you out. I *need* you to do this."

Kuini blinked. "I don't understand, Father."

"There is nothing to understand. You and I seem to be the only Highlanders sharing that strange sentiment, seeing the danger at having the Tepanecs next to our mountains. I can do my best here, while you and your friend will be able to do better elsewhere." The palm resting on Kuini's shoulder tightened. "In Tenochtitlan there are people who are working to that end, and you and your highborn Acolhua can help, probably more than you, or even them, can imagine."

"Tenochtitlan? But Father, the Aztecs betrayed the Acolhua people, they are siding with the Tepanecs now. Of all places, they were the ones to receive Texcoco as their tributary, to make the Lowlanders pay them a heavy tribute. They are the part of the Tepanec Empire, coming there willingly and oh-so-very humbly. We will be of no use in Tenochtitlan, and Coyotl's life will be in greater danger the moment he crosses their waters."

The firm arm propelled him back down the road. "There is no time to discuss it tonight. I talked to your friend, and if that cracked head of his did not make him forget, he'll be able to explain it to you in a good time." He measured the sky. "It's well past midnight, and we should go back and see how fast you two can be organized."

But Kuini refused to move. "Father, I'm not leaving! If saving the heir to the Texcoco throne seems important to you, then let Coyotl go to Tenochtitlan. But I will not leave you here with all this trouble on your hands. You will be held responsible for our flight. You will be accused of all sorts of things, and this time your enemies will be partly correct." He stood the penetrating gaze. "I will go after the meeting of the council."

"The meeting of the council will not discuss you. They would wish to discuss the Lowlander and his crimes. Yours are not that significant."

"Still, I'm staying." Feeling childish and unreasonable, he stood the heavy gaze. Whichever were this wise man's reasons, he knew, he would regret agreeing to leave. His father was a great leader and his ability to express himself, his logical thinking, his forceful presence were usually such that they made people follow. But he would not succumb, not this time. He had ruined it all, and he needed to stay to face the consequences.

Clenching his fists, he stared at the weathered face, seeing the lips quivering, fighting a smile. Then the hearty laughter broke the night.

"You are impossible, Son. Plain impossible. Wild beasts of the Underworld would be unable to stop you when you decided to leave against any better judgment. And this time those beasts would be defeated once again now that you decided to stay, contradicting again any logic and reason." The laughter subdued, turning into a wide smile. "Do not mistake me. I do understand your reasons. You want to help me face the problem you believe you created. But you are wrong. The Tepanecs and the foolish Lowlanders were the ones creating our problems, while you brought here the partial solution. If someone else had come here with the Lowlander heir, I would have acted quite the same. This opportunity is too good to miss. As it is, you happened to do this, and I'm glad one of my sons turned out to be so brave and farsighted." The smile widened, reaching the dark eyes. "You make me proud. Other people may not see it yet, but they will. They will be honored to be led by you one day, should you want to lead anyone." Turning away, he began walking the moonlit road. "But now let us hurry."

Upon reaching the house, the man halted once again.

"Your friend will need you. He may not be able to survive Tenochtitlan without your active help. Your connections in this *altepetl* so far are infinitely better. You have no enemies there, while the Lowlander will be in quite a danger, in the beginning at least." A proud smile flashed. "In Tenochtitlan, you have a powerful uncle, the former Warlord, the man who liked and appreciated you for what you are before he knew of your family connections. You will have to make it work between those two, the Texcoco heir and the former Warlord. According to your friend, they didn't get along well before."

Kuini found it difficult to suppress a chuckle.

"No, they did not," he said, remembering the Texcoco Palace and the hot afternoon when Coyotl tried to "save" him, Kuini, from the arrogant Aztec. It would be good to see this man, wouldn't it? And hadn't he wanted to go to Tenochtitlan anyway? He hesitated. "But Father, what will you do? You'll be accused of letting us go against the direct orders of the town's council. They will not let it pass unnoticed, not with your enemies so battle-hungry and eager for your blood."

The man shook his head. "I won't be set aside that easily. I still have much influence and many powerful friends. You've seen it in the council today. Aside from some petty discontents, people trust me." Smile wide and unreserved, the man proceeded toward the house, radiating cheerful forcefulness, as if having not a worry in the whole world. "I can deal with our people. And without you two around to make everyone angry, I'll be able to do it more easily, come to think of it." The glittering eyes measured Kuini, amused. "Isn't that what you wanted to suggest when you came to see me on the night before?"

"Yes, I did. How did you know?"

"Your friend told me. We gossiped about you this morning."

Fighting a smile, Kuini hesitated. "Thank you, Father. Thank you for everything. I don't know what I did to earn this honor, to have such a great man for a father, but I will try to live up to it. I will do my best to make you proud, to live up to your expectations."

The man's smile did not waver. "You are already doing that, Son."

Mino stood at the doorway, watching them coming down the path. They didn't seem like father and son, so different in their appearance and their bearing; and yet, they looked so much alike now, walking together, their paces confident and long.

She took a deep breath and blinked away the wetness that suddenly blurred her vision. They were walking together, talking, at long last. Oh, how she had longed for this to happen, how afraid she had been thinking that this moment would never come. Clasping her palms tight, she returned their smiles as they neared.

"How is the Lowlander?" inquired her husband, halting beside her, his smile wide, eyes bright, unconcerned.

"He is back among the living. I'm not certain he is fit for a long journey, but having no choice…" She shook her head. "He would recover better if he had some rest and some medicine for the next few dawns."

Her husband frowned. "They don't have a few dawns. They'll have to take their chances, and you can pack an ointment for them to take along together with food and things."

"I can't pack an ointment. It should be freshly prepared." She shrugged. "And there is still a danger he'll get sick because of the wound. It's quite open, you know."

"But he came back to his senses, didn't he?" asked Kuini, obviously relieved.

"Yes, he did. You can go in and talk to him."

His smile wide, revealing a row of large white teeth with a gap of one missing, her son beamed at her. "Then all is well. I know a girl who will be able to help us, to take care of him until he is better. Don't pack the medicine, but throw in more food, would you?"

She saw her husband turning to watch him, as puzzled as she was. Kuini's happy smile did not waver.

"I know of a suitable person, that's all," he said finally, grinning back, looking unconcerned.

"Here in the Highlands?"

"Yes, here in your realm. We'll have to detour through the Tlaxcala Valley, but we will reach our destination eventually, and by then Coyotl will be as good as new."

She opened her mouth to ask as to the nature of that mysterious place, or a girl, but her husband's palm wrapped around her shoulders, turning her gently, propelling her back inside the house. "I'm sure he knows what he is doing," he said, squeezing her in his warm embrace. "So let us just get those two organized."

The Lowlander sat upright, leaning against the wall, pressing a soaked, smelly cloth to his forehead. He did, indeed, look better now, with his slender face pale but not lifeless, not the way he had looked when arriving here earlier. His eyes lit up when he saw Kuini, and he leaned forward, swaying, but holding on. How would her son manage to take this youth even as far as that mysterious place toward the Tlaxcala Valley?

For another heartbeat, she watched them talking quietly, then went to organize their bags. Blankets, she thoughts, lots of blankets, and a pair of good cloaks and loincloths, and food.

She piled in all the dried meat left from the Cold Moons, then threw in tortillas and all her stocks of dried and fresh fruits and berries. Tenochtitlan was not that far away but for their proposed detour into the Tlaxcala Valley. Who knew how long they'd be roaming the countryside, hiding from their own people.

Shivering, she leaned against the wooden chest, shutting her eyes for a heartbeat. No matter how her husband chose to present his solution to the troublesome situation, the youths were fleeing, escaping the town under the cover of the night. Whatever the future held for them all, they were in serious trouble now, her son and his friend, and more than anyone – her husband.

She glanced at him as he squatted upon the mat, talking calmly, unhurriedly, radiating authority. As expected, she saw both youths listening avidly, afraid to miss a word. Oh, but he was used to this kind of attention. People tended to listen to him, to trust him, to follow him readily. He had so many good ideas and his confidence knew no bounds. And yet...

Would his brilliance help him tomorrow, when he'd have to face the town's elders and the rest of his peers? How would he explain that the youths trusted into his care, his responsibility, went away with his ardent consent? He would not lie, she knew, wringing her hands, biting her lips into a raw mess. He would tell them exactly what happened and why. He had never bothered to be anything but himself, trusting people to appreciate his reasons.

Clenching her teeth, she studied the patterns on a pottery bowl full of dried berries she held. What did she intend to do with it? Her gaze brushed past the bags. Oh, the boys. They could use some dried fruits. It was a good thing to carry when journeying.

She heard his voice as it floated in the semidarkness. Not trying to understand his words, she just listened, seeking reassurance. He looked vital, purposeful, calm and confident, but animated, almost excited, younger than his years once again. How could he be so lighthearted about it? Didn't he understand the seriousness of the situation? Did his confidence know no bounds?

Oh, he will lose his position, she knew, her palms sweaty and sleek against each other. And with no trust from the town's elders, with enemies like disgusting Ai, who knew what else he may lose? Might his life be in danger?

She saw him leaning forward, explaining, gesturing, his eyes alight. Watching his straight shoulders, his rough, weathered palms relaxed in his lap, his whole posture radiating lightness and well being, she felt her taut nerves calming down as well. He looked in peace with his world, at long last. He hadn't looked like that for a very long time. All this because of his youngest son?

Her eyes shifted toward Kuini as the youth asked something, his handsome, broad Tepanec face alight and free of shadows as well. She hadn't seen him so calm and confident since, oh, since before these few stormy days, three summers ago, when he came back from his wild adventures in the Lowlands for the first time. He had so much of his father in him, she realized, suddenly feeling lighthearted. And he was happy now too, happy and relieved. He had found direction in life.

Feeling her smile spreading, she busied herself searching for more foodstuff. Oh yes, these two men of hers would find the way. They would deal with this trouble, and then, they would find how to throw the Tepanecs back to their side of the Great Lake.

She glanced at the Lowlander, wishing to laugh all of a sudden. Had she just treated the future Emperor of Texcoco and the five Acolhua provinces? Shrugging, she fought her grin from spreading. She'd come a long way since being brought to Texcoco as a captured girl to be sold into slavery more than twice twenty summers ago. And here she was, giving the future Acolhua Emperor his life back again.

The ways of the gods *were* strange, stranger than the wildest imagination of a mad storyteller, she thought, tucking the whole bowl of dried berries into one of the bags. Yes, the boys would make their journey, and they would succeed in re-shaping the future of the whole Great Lake and all lands around it.

EPILOGUE

Crouching behind the low bushes, Dehe counted her heartbeats, afraid to breathe. No sound disturbed the silence, still she could not gather enough courage to leave the safety of her hiding place, to peek again through the half shuttered opening in the wall.

She had nearly been caught when she did it last time, many hundreds of heartbeats before, when the house went quiet for enough time to make her feel confident. Still, when she had peeked inside the spacious room, contemplating the manner of sneaking in, a relatively young woman was just rising from her mat, looking straight toward that same wall opening, or so it seemed.

The silence enveloped her, so deep it felt like no living creature was left alive. No insects buzzed, no breeze rustled in the bushes, no night creature sneaked around. The world went dead.

Clutching the small bag in her sweat-soaked palm, Dehe counted another hundred heartbeats. She had to go out and check the wall opening again. It was either that or to go back to the safety of her woods, back to her cave, to pack and leave, knowing that *he* would not be coming to take her away, knowing that she had left and did not look back when *he* was in trouble.

Clasping her lips tight, she slipped out, leaving the safety of her cover. This time the room appeared quiet and dark, with faint shapes of people sleeping upon the mats. That same young woman and two children. All three could wake up easily, yet there were no other invitingly open shutters. She had inspected the rest of the walls before.

Twisting carefully, she sneaked in, thanking the Green-Skirt

Goddess for keeping her so small and thin. A little wider in the hips and she would have never managed. Suppressing the suddenness of her smile, she remembered how his rough, weathered palms looked so enormously large against her body, wandering it in those beautiful, exciting ways. Oh, she was a woman now, not a small insignificant girl. And she would save him.

Taking a deep breath, she left the relative safety of the window, slipping carefully along the wall, away from the curling figures and toward the inner doorway. In the next room, two middle-aged women slept one near another, covered by embroidered blankets. Shifting her eyes, lest her gaze would awake them in some way, she looked around, taking in the tidiness and the spaciousness of the room. Mats were piled in the far corner, arranged neatly next to the low table, clean and covered with colorful cloth.

Frowning, Dehe headed for another doorway. She needed to hurry, and her courage was leaving her again.

Clenching her teeth, she entered the next room and stopped dead in her tracks, her heart thumping. Now that she had reached her destination, she felt her limbs going liquid, refusing to obey her. Her eyes glued to the man sleeping on the soft blankets, she tried to slam her mind into working, hardly registering the young woman sleeping next to him.

Why had she come here? What was she thinking?

She watched the man's bony hands spread to his sides, remembering the way those palms had dug into her shoulder when he chased her through the woods, his face sweaty and twisted, eyes blazing with anger. He would have killed her if he had managed to catch her, because she had overheard him plotting against the War Leader. Oh yes, he would not hesitate. And now, here she was, about to kill him instead, because his plans somehow worked, against her timely warning.

Oh, why hadn't she persuaded *him* to stay and not to go back to the town? Why hadn't she thought about it? He was so short-tempered, so easily aroused. Of course he had gotten into trouble. Even the most placid people could be provoked if pushed skillfully.

She felt her anger rising, and it gave her enough strength to tear her eyes off the sleeping couple. A quick glance around told her that this room was less spacious, but as generously furnished. Also, this time, there was a flask on the low table. Oh, the goddess was watching over her.

Her bag clutched tightly in her hand, Dehe slipped toward the pile of mats, keeping away from the curling figures. It took her what seemed like ages to untie the maguey strings. Her fingers trembled so badly, she almost spilled the brownish powder all over the floor. Some of it scattered upon the table, and she bit her lips to stop herself from cursing aloud.

Breathing quietly, she scooped the brownish mess into her trembling palms, then sniffed the contents of the flask. *Pulque*, no doubt. Good. The spicy drink was better than water, its strong taste and distinctive aroma more likely to conceal the other presence and the slight aftertaste.

Carefully, she shook the powder off her palms, directing the brownish dust into the narrow beak. It floated near the surface, so she stirred it with her finger until the thick beverage seemed to return to its previous milky state.

Encouraged and feeling much better, she glanced at the sleeping figures again. It would be safer to search for the man's dagger and just stab him. He may not wish to drink the *pulque* first thing in the morning, and until he did, someone else might drink it, finishing the whole thing.

Oh Green-Skirt Goddess, she thought, *please let this man drink it. Don't let him live any longer. I will keep your altar covered in flowers for many seasons, I promise you that!* She would need to find the appropriate temple as soon as she got to her beloved Tlaxcala Valley. As soon as *he* took her there.

Tying her bag carefully, she made sure the table was clean and the flask upon it looked untouched. No, she could not risk the whole thing by trying to stab the vile man. He was a hunter, with the strength and the instincts of such. Her chances of killing him this way were slim, while the poisonous drink should do the work. Even if someone else drank from it, he was still likely to get his share. A cup or so would be more than enough.

Shrugging, she glanced at the sleeping woman. What if someone else got hurt? Well, she needed to ensure the safety of her man. His father clearly meant much to him, therefore she would help the renowned leader as well. The Warriors' Leader would benefit from her deed, more than his son even.

Creeping alongside the coolness of the wall, she felt her excitement welling. Whatever the trouble was, they'd be able to deal with it now that the most bitter enemy of his father would soon be dead. And then he would come and take her away, and maybe she'd be able to persuade him to stay with her somewhere around the Tlaxcala Valley. Oh, they would have such a nice life together.

Outside once again, breathing the fresh nightly air with enjoyment, she fought the impulse to go to his father's house again. But oh no, she said to herself. It was not wise. It might get her into trouble. She had overheard enough of his conversation with his father and the annoying priestess to know he'd be heading her way and soon.

No, she thought, shaking her head. She'd go back to her place, and she'd wait for him there. He would come, and if he decided to go elsewhere, not to settle in the depths of the Tlaxcala Valley, well, then she'd go with him.

She pitted her face against the soft breeze, fighting her smile from spreading. No, she would not let him leave her. Whatever his plans were, she would find a way to make him keep her as his woman.

AUTHOR'S AFTERWORD

In 1419, having conquered Texcoco and its provinces, the Tepanecs were the undeniable masters of the whole Mexican Valley, spreading further and further, strong and invincible. Curiously indifferent, they took the coastal Acolhua towns, including Coatlinchan, but according to some primary sources, the *altepetl* of Texcoco they had given to their worthwhile allies, the Aztecs of Tenochtitlan.

Nezahualcoyotl's flight into the Highlands is a tale in itself, described in generous detail by the 17th century Acolhua most prominent annalist Fernando Ixtlilxochitl, and in less detail by Diego Duran and Domingo Chimalpahin. Some sources claim that the Acolhua heir fled as far as the Tlaxcala Valley, but others name the geographically closer Huexotzinco, which indeed provided the future Texcoco ruler with generous amount of warriors when the time to rebel against the might of the Tepanecs came.

However, no rebellion happened while Tezozomoc, the old Tepanec ruler, lived and ruled, having seen well over hundred years according to several claims. His death was imminent and there were many who awaited this event with eagerness.

In Tenochtitlan, the opinions varied. While benefiting from its newly gained stance with their mighty overlords, having received the rich Acolhua *altepetl* as a gift for their good behavior, some of the leading Aztecs were not happy with the way their city was turning into yet another Tepanec province. The rich pickings may not have been worth the loss of independence.

Most primary sources agree that young Nezahualcoyotl did not spend too much time in the Highlands, coming to live in Tenochtitlan instead, having its young ruler Chimalpopoca interceding before Tezozomoc on his behalf. Busy expanding their city, building another causeway and the water construction, the Aztecs still tried to keep the Tepanecs happy, but it all was destined to change.

What happened next can be read in the third book of "The Rise of the Aztecs Series", **"The Emperor's Second Wife."**

The story continues with

THE EMPEROR'S SECOND WIFE

The Rise of the Aztecs, Book 3

PROLOGUE

Tenochtitlan, 1417
Before the second Tepanec invasion of Texcoco

Iztac eyed the large rubber ball wide-eyed, rolling it between her palms.

"Where did you get this?" she asked the boy, not taking her eyes off the rare object. Tossing it in the air, she caught it back with difficulty. The ball was heavy and unpleasantly coarse.

The boy's eyes sparked. "You'll never guess."

"Oh, yes?" She looked at him, taking in the gentle face, the yet-uncut hair, the slender form of a boy eleven summers old, too small for his years. "Let me think. You went out for *calmecac* lessons this morning. So you must have found it somewhere along the road." She wrinkled her nose. "I wish I could get out of the Palace too, sometimes."

"Such a ball? Along the road? Can't happen!" called her young companion, victorious. "Do you think those things are just rolling all over the city?" Pointedly, he rolled his eyes "Haven't you seen a ball game in your life?"

"I've seen many ball games!" exclaimed Iztac hotly. "In Texcoco we have a beautiful court, as large as this whole palace. I watched that game twenty times and more. You don't have such things in Tenochtitlan."

The boy frowned. "I've seen warriors playing more than your twenty times." He watched her as she tossed the round object once again, catching it with both arms. "You can't touch it with your hands."

"I know that." She threw the ball, then tried to hit it with her elbow. It slipped off and rolled over the ground. The boy's laughter made her angry. "You can't do any better," she said, kicking the ball impatiently.

"Oh, yes, I can." He picked it up, then proceeded to throw it in his turn. His sandaled foot shot sideways, hitting the ball with his hip, sending it back into the air.

Iztac gasped. "I can't believe it. How did you do this?"

"Easily." His eyes sparkled.

"Do it again!"

This time he missed, cursed, picked up the ball anew. She caught her breath, wishing him to succeed. He was so vulnerable, so unsure of himself, this heir to the Aztec throne. Just a boy of a little over eleven summers, kind and well-meaning, with no streak of viciousness to his nature, not a natural warrior. He was as nice as his father, but having a fierce, dominant woman for a mother was his bad luck, decided Iztac, watching the ball flying sideways after a less successful toss of an elbow.

"Let me try," she said, grabbing the coarse rubber as it rolled over the ground again. "Where did you learn to do this?"

"There was this man in *calmecac* this morning. The other boys say he is coming there to teach every few dawns now. He is so old!" The boy rolled his eyes. "He said the warriors should know how to handle a ball, so he took us outside and proceeded to show us." His hands flopped in the air. "Iztac-Ayotl, you wouldn't believe it. He is so old, but he ran and hit the ball with all parts of his body. He made all the boys work. But I was the best. Would you believe that? I did better than the rest of them!" He beamed at her, his pride spilling over.

She hugged him. "Oh, Chimal, I'm so proud of you!"

His shoulders were thin, fragile against her touch. He needed to develop his arms, she reflected. At his age, *calmecac* boys were supposed to be stronger, more fit. Why wouldn't his mother let him join the school like a regular boy?

"So, did this man cut his lessons short when it became too hot?" she asked, moving away and picking up the ball again.

His face fell. "No. They went on. Then he said they would practice shooting slings." He glanced at the sky. "I suppose they are doing it now."

She kicked the ball angrily. "Why won't they let you attend *calmecac* like a normal boy?"

He shrugged. "Because I will be the emperor."

"It's not an excuse. My brother will also be an emperor, and he went to *calmecac* for many summers. Like you, he attended the lessons, but when he was about your age he went to live in *calmecac* like any other boy."

"Well, your Acolhua people are strange," he said haughtily. "My mother says the future emperor should not mingle with his subjects. She says the emperor can't be treated like a simple warrior. She says they should not be allowed to talk to me like any other boy."

"Well, then, here you are, stuck in the Palace with no ballgames." She saw his face twisting, and regretted her outburst. He was just a boy, and she was a grown woman of seventeen summers, the Emperor's Second Wife. She was not a girl anymore, and this place was not the Texcocan Palace, this boy not her brother to mess around with, and laugh and tease with no mercy.

She clenched her teeth against the memories. It pounced on her suddenly, as it always would, threatening to take her, to shatter her oh-so-painfully erected walls of oblivion. Texcoco and its Palace, the place she had loathed so much, the place she had thought to be her prison, now loomed in her memory, beautiful and imposing, perfectly groomed, with her trustworthy maids and all that freedom to run about, away from the watchful eyes of her father, the Emperor, or his Second Wife, her mother, having her brother, the best boy in the whole world, for a friend.

She remembered herself complaining to Coyotl that she was just a meaningless princess. Well, now she knew better. What a delightful existence it was, to be just one of many, to matter to no one. Only as the Second Wife of the Emperor had she had discovered what real imprisonment was.

She took a deep breath. *Stop being such a whiny cihua,* she admonished herself. *You can still sneak to the Palace's gardens whenever you like, and you have this boy to play with, if occasionally. Or play with a ball, like now.*

"Come," she said, snatching the ball back from his hands. "Show me how you do this. Stop pulling those offended faces. You are not the emperor yet."

"And you are not the first wife," he retorted, lips pursed.

"And I will never be this thing. And I don't want it, either. It's such a bore!"

"No, it's not. Chief wives can order everyone about. No one dares to argue with my mother, ever."

Iztac shivered. "Well, your mother makes a good Empress. Of course everyone obeys her."

Even the Emperor himself, she reflected, her stomach twisting uneasily. Oh, but she made such tremendous efforts to avoid getting in the way of this terrible woman.

She shivered again, remembering the first time she had seen Tenochtitlan's Empress, tall and widely built, with her broad face and large, widely spaced eyes, so typical of the Tepanecs. One of Tezozomoc's favorite daughters, given to the Aztec Emperor as a token of good faith. To make sure Tenochtitlan behaved, was Iztac's private conclusion. Such an imposing, domineering, fierce woman. Not that she had noticed any of that at first.

Her arrival at Tenochtitlan had swept by, vague and bleary, like a bad dream. She remembered only the fragments of it. The damp air that assaulted her nostrils, the dismal looking palace with no resemblance to the richness of the Texcoco Emperor's dwelling, the pleasant looking face of Huitzilihuitl, the Emperor, smiling at her, his eyebrows raised in surprise, saying something about her beauty and charm.

She remembered herself breathing with relief when she had finally been led to a private set of rooms, away from the multitude of people that studied her as though she were an exotic animal from the thickness of the highland forests. The Highlands! She remembered battling the tears, keeping them at bay. She would not cry, not in front of those people, nor in the privacy of her rooms.

Well, those were not her rooms, she was quick to discover.

Those were the Emperor's rooms. As the maids rushed to and fro, busy removing her imposing headdress and some of the heaviest jewelry, she had breathed with relief. It was so good to be rid of its crushing weight. But when they began painting her cheeks and lips, dressing her in a light, flimsy robe tied by a colorful girdle, a new wave of latent fear washed through her. Their smiles and giggles told her what would be the last part of the ceremony. She thought of the Emperor's hands removing the light material, and her stomach twisted so violently, she became sick, and the maids hurried to replace the ruined garment with another one.

Smiling grimly, she remembered that she had been spared that part of the ceremony, after all. Huddled in a far corner, with the maids distressed and uncomfortable, she had shut her eyes at the sound of many footsteps, but the commanding voice of a woman was the one to interrupt the sudden silence.

"Out. All of you," said the woman imperiously. "Wait at the outer corridor until I call."

The feathers on the delicate headdress of the Empress rustled angrily as the maids and the servants scattered through the doorway. Iztac just stared, mesmerized by the broad face and the large, slightly squinted eyes that gazed at her with the coldness and calm of an ocelot eyeing a forest mouse. Not a decent meal for a predator, but a disturbance nevertheless.

"Get up, girl," said the woman coldly, when the last of the servants was safely away and the room went eerily quiet. "Take a seat over there, on this chair by the podium."

Fighting to get to her feet, Iztac made a tremendous effort not to drop her gaze.

"I think it's time we have our first talk." The woman neared the opposite chair and set there, majestic, the richly embroidered rims of her gown rustling. "Two noble wives of a noble emperor." She grinned coldly. "Huitzilihuitl has many wives, but none of them matter. They are not noble enough, and they are not important." Her gaze grew colder, more difficult to stand. "Well, little princess of Texcoco, how was your journey?"

Iztac cleared her throat, trying to say something. Nothing came out.

"Oh, girl, don't be so frightened," said the woman, but her eyes flickered with satisfaction, telling Iztac that if she was frightened now, she didn't know yet what real fright was. "We can get along. You seem to be a nice little thing. You won't stand in my way, will you?"

Iztac clasped her palms to stop them from trembling, but even the pain of her nails sinking into her flesh did not help. Her mind refused to suggest any kind of an answer, even had her lips been able to form the words.

"You see," went on the woman, unabashed by the lack of response. "There can be only one empress, so it's important that you should not nurture any ideas of you becoming one. You have the necessary blood, and you have looks." The woman leaned forward, placing her well groomed palms upon the reed podium between them. "I would hate to see such a pretty girl getting hurt. Your mother is one of my half sisters, another daughter of my father, the mighty Emperor of Azcapotzalco. Your father, the Emperor of Texcoco, was foolish enough to replace her with another Chief Wife, a sister of my husband." The woman shook her head. "Oh, how foolish of him. Texcoco will lose this war. The Tepanecs will take this *altepetl* and the rest of the Acolhua lands. But my father would rule it wisely, better than your father did."

The thought of the Tepanecs swarming Texcoco shores, the thought of Coyotl and the nearing battle, helped.

"My people will not lose," said Iztac, surprised by the clearness of her voice. "They will throw the Tepanecs back into the Great Lake, and then they will cross it to conquer Azcapotzalco itself."

The derisive grin disappeared. "Oh, you are a spirited one. I see." The dark eyes grew freezing cold. "Listen, girl. I didn't come here to talk politics. You are nothing but an insignificant princess, just another one of the minor wives. You understand little, if anything. It would not be appropriate for me, the Chief Wife and the Empress, to spend my time lecturing you on history and politics." The feathers rustled again as the woman tossed her head high. "I came to tell you this, and I will not be repeating myself. You are to stay at the minor wives quarters, and you are not to pursue the Emperor with any of your girlish tricks. He may honor you with an occasional visit, but you are not to bear him a child." The eyes bored into her, now blazing, burning her skin. "Should you conceive, you will not be allowed to bring this child into our Fifth World. You will be dead long before it happens."

Iztac felt her heart, which had been pounding wildly, going still. Like a wave traveling through her chest, it slipped down her stomach, leaving everything gray, lifeless, dead in its wake. She clutched the uneven surface of the reed podium with both hands, her anger rising, sudden and difficult to control.

"I will take my own life before you have the pleasure of killing me," she said hoarsely. "But I will not do this until I hear of my people's great victories, until I hear how they ruined Azcapotzalco, until I know what tribute they've made the Tepanecs pay." The woman's face swam before her eyes and she blinked, desperate to banish the tears. These were of rage, not of fear, but she was afraid the woman would interpret them wrongly. "I will not bear *your* Emperor a son. If I can help it, he will never touch me at all. If you can make him not come to me at nights, I would be grateful. I don't want to be his Chief Wife. All I want is to go home. All I want is to go away, to run as far as the Smoking Mountain of the Highlands, if you wish to know. I don't want your place, and I don't want your status. And I will take my own life, but not before I hear of my people's victories."

She shut her eyes, her heart pumping insanely, as if trying to jump out of her chest, like the heart of a sacrificial victim.

"Oh, what a spirited girl you are." The woman's voice reached her, overcoming the pounding in her ears. "I would hate to see you suffer. I would hate to have to get rid of you. The Tepanec blood of your mother is raging in your veins, that much is obvious. You may feel loyal to your Acolhua side, but you are a Tepanec in your spirit." Pausing, the woman smiled coldly, then rose to her feet. "We may come to know each other well over the future summers. If you behave, those may even be pleasant encounters for you. Remember what I said. You bear no children to the Emperor, and you keep away from him." A cold grin flashed fleetingly. "As a favor from a woman to a woman, I'll make sure he doesn't come to you tonight. You will be removed from these premises shortly, oh proud Acolhua princess. It'll be off to the minor wives quarters for you, to share it with the rest of the insignificant women."

The light paces dimmed, disappearing down the corridor. Iztac shut her eyes once again. She tried to take deep breaths, but they came in with difficulty, convulsive, bringing no relief. The fact that the Emperor would not come to her tonight rang in her ears again and again. He would not be untying the ropes of her gown.

She clasped her palms tight. Oh, the gods were so kind to her.

The memory of the moonlit grass around the pond surfaced, the memory she had managed to tuck away for the past market interval, since her last attempt to find *him* on the Plaza. The memory of his large brown hands, rough and scratched, the hands of a youth used to fighting and climbing, doing all sorts of wild things, yet their fingers long and well-shaped, the fingers of a man good at drawing and painting. Oh, he drew such beautiful pictures. And he had taken his time untying her robe, she remembered, although it would have been enough just to pull the light gown up.

The moon goddess, she thought. *Revered and silvery, but golden for him, with obsidian for eyes.* She sobbed and let the wave of grief take her. Now the tears flowed unrestrained, and she didn't care anymore.

"Iztac-Ayotl, wake up!"

The boy's voice tore her out of her reverie, brought her back to the clear afternoon sky and the rustling trees of the Palace's gardens, two summers later.

"You look like you've just seen a ghost!" He peered at her teasingly. "Have you?"

"No. I was remembering what it was like when I first arrived here."

"Oh, I remember you well." He pulled a face. "You were sparkling like a statue, and you looked like you would faint at any moment."

"I did not!"

"Oh yes, you did. You were so frightened. Like a girl. And you are a girl, a silly girl."

She measured him with a glance full of meaning. "Don't you mess with me, Chimalpopoca."

He giggled, then sobered abruptly. "I'm not saying you are frightened now. But you were back then, all the same." He frowned. "I felt bad for you."

"No, I wasn't." She snatched the ball from his hands. "But I will fall asleep if you don't start playing. Show me everything that this old warrior taught you."

"He is not just an old warrior. He was our Chief Warlord for, oh, ages."

"Oh, the Aztec Chief Warlord! I should have guessed." She drew her breath sharply. *More ghosts from the past.*

"What? What's wrong with him?"

"Nothing. It doesn't matter. Everything is wrong with him. I hate him."

"Why?"

She ground her teeth. "He kidnapped someone. Someone I knew."

Chimal burst out laughing. "Chief warlords don't kidnap people. No one can tell them 'no,' anyway. No one but the emperor," he corrected himself. "Chief warlords take warriors and go out and kill our enemies. You are so silly."

"Yes, I know what warlords do. But he did kidnap this boy all the same." She saw him opening his mouth to argue and plugged her ears with her hands. "I don't what to talk about it, so don't even try! And anyway, why hasn't he died already? He is so old."

"He is not that old. They say he is like three times twenty summers old or something. I've seen people older than him. And he is hopping all over the place. He is teaching history and warfare, but they say he is too eager to get to the training grounds and give them actual lessons on all sorts of weapons." He sighed. "I wish I was allowed to live in *calmecac* like the rest of the boys."

She watched his twisting face, her chest filling with compassion, pushing her own misery away. "Maybe we should try to talk to the Emperor. He is your father after all. And he is the Emperor."

His dubious glance made her hold her tongue. Huitzilihuitl

was a kind, pleasant sort of a man, wise and far-sighted. He made good laws, and he judged wisely in the imperial court. He strove to achieve his goals peacefully whatever the cost, avoiding struggles and confrontations. He gave up on the argument with his advisers when they maintained that the cost of building a special construction to bring fresh water to Tenochtitlan would be too high. He never argued with their Tepanec overlords. He had preferred to abandon his Acolhua allies, instead. He never argued with his powerful Chief Wife, either.

"I'll try to talk to him about you when he sends for me," she said resolutely.

"Does he see you in private?"

"Sometimes."

She thought about the rare occasions on which the Emperor would send for her, to be brought into his chambers, quietly and hurriedly, as if by stealth. He would look at her guiltily, as though regretting not being able to do it more often. Not wasting his time on talking, he would take her gently and carefully, only to send her away afterward. Neither pleased, nor repulsed, she would leave, breathing with relief, afraid of only one thing – that she may be with child. However, those encounters were infrequent, occurring only once in every few moons, and so far, she hadn't conceived.

That was no lovemaking on either part, she knew. It was a physical act, but for what purpose, she didn't know, didn't care to ask. The lovemaking belonged to the past, to the silvery night and the moonlit pond.

She clenched her teeth tight and forced her mind to focus on the boy, who seemed to be studying her carefully.

"The Emperor sent for me about a market interval ago and this time he wanted to talk," she said, forcing a smile. "So maybe I'll be able to talk to him about you the next time."

The boy frowned. "Doesn't he talk to you every time he sends for you?"

"No. He doesn't talk to me."

"What does he do to you?"

She shifted her weight from one foot to another. "All sorts of things. The things men do to their wives." Uncomfortable under his heavy gaze, she added hurriedly, trying to clear the atmosphere. "He doesn't think I know enough history or politics." She winked. "I haven't attended *calmecac,* either."

"But you did your temple training. All girls do this." He looked away, frowning. "When I'm the Emperor, I'll take you to be my Chief Wife."

She laughed. "I'm too old for you. But your mother will find you the prettiest princess in the entire valley. And the noblest one. Well, anyway, I didn't do my temple training, either," she added in order to change the subject, unsettled by the anger flashing out of his eyes. "Texcoco was busy preparing to fight the Tepanecs back then, so they never got around sending me to the temples."

The pleasant face of Tenochtitlan's future ruler twisted. "Stupid Acolhua Emperor."

"He is not stupid! He beat off the Tepanec invasion, and then he invaded their lands. He beat them three times in three large battles! Think about it. He took towns and villages." She flapped her hands in the air. "He laid a siege to Azcapotzalco itself!"

The boy's eyes flashed. "But he didn't succeed. He took his warriors and ran back to his side of the Great Lake."

"So what? He will regroup, and the Tepanecs will think twice before trying to attack Texcoco again."

But as she said that, she knew it was not true. The Tepanec Emperor enlisted the support of more *altepetls,* even of his old enemies from the towns around Lake Chalco. He was preparing another invasion as they spoke, here in the tranquility of the Tenochtitlan Palace, neutral and perfectly safe. That was what Huitzilihuitl had told her when he had sent for her a market interval ago.

She frowned, remembering how surprised she had been, bidden to sit alongside the Emperor's chair – not the magnificent chair of the main hall, but a pretty affair, nevertheless. Not daring to touch the offered refreshments, she glanced at the pleasant-looking face of her husband, a man she hardly knew, a stranger. He looked tired and not at his best. Dark rings surrounded his eyes, and the narrow face had a grayish shade to it.

Uncomfortable, she had listened to him as he talked at length about his Acolhua allies, about his responsibilities to his growing *altepetl* and his Mexica people, about his obligations to Azcapotzalco. The man seemed troubled, and as if in a bad need to talk.

"Your people have proven brave and resourceful," he concluded. "How can one watch the struggle of the worthwhile neighbors and allies without offering help?"

Pondering this obviously rhetorical question, she watched him, swept with compassion. He was a nice man, and he seemed to feel bad for not joining the Texcoco people in their struggle. Tenochtitlan would benefit from taking the Tepanecs down. Thanks to the haughty Empress and her connection in the Tepanec Capital, Tenochtitlan's tribute was not heavy. Still, a tribute was a tribute. But then, Tenochtitlan had benefited from the continued hostilities of its neighbors as well. The traffic of the canoes around their shores grew, with the traders trying to avoid the troublesome areas, detouring through the Aztec island, instead.

Hugging her elbows, she said nothing.

"Shall I help your father, Iztac-Ayotl?" asked the Emperor finally, gaze nearly imploring.

"Yes, I think you should," she whispered, unsure of herself. She cleared her throat. "I think none of our *altepetls* should pay a tribute to the Tepanecs."

He shook his head. "I wish it was that simple!"

"But maybe it is, Revered Emperor," she said, feeling the calm flowing through her body. "Your Chief Wife is the favorite daughter of the Tepanec Emperor, but your sister is the favorite wife of my father, the Acolhua Emperor. He put aside his own Tepanec Empress to favor your sister." She allowed herself a tiny smile. "You are obliged to your both neighbors, but while one is aggressive and demanding, the other is fighting a war on behalf of both our *altepetls*."

A smiled dawned. "You are a wise woman, Second Wife. How old are you?"

"I've seen seventeen summers."

"You are wiser than your years warrant."

She shifted uneasily, aware of the servants. What if someone reported this conversation to the Empress?

He capped his forehead with both palms. "I may do this, you know. I cannot stand on the side any longer. Tezozomoc had demanded our active participation this time, and I cannot do this. I cannot betray my Acolhua allies."

She shivered despite the afternoon heat. "Are the Tepanecs going to invade Texcoco again?"

"Yes," he said. "And this time they will be better prepared."

Clasping her palms tight, feeling them sleek and sweaty against each other, she remembered Coyotl's face glimmering with excitement as he had told her that they were going to beat the Tepanecs, beaming at her, glowing with pride, brave and invincible. They did beat the Tepanecs back then. Already in Tenochtitlan, deep in her private misery, she remembered how excited she had become, for a few heartbeats at least, warmed by the wonderful news; how she had wished she could see her brother in order to tell him how proud she was. Then, there was more news of Acolhua forces crossing the Great Lake, invading the towns belonging to the Tepanecs. Somewhat accustomed to her new life by then, already being friends with Chimal, she contemplated sending a note to Coyotl, somehow. He had promised to come to Tenochtitlan, to visit her, hadn't he? She could barely contain her excitement back then. It would be so wonderful to see him victorious. Well, it would be so wonderful to see him no matter how.

Coming back from her reverie, she grinned at the boy. "I'll talk to the Emperor. He is sure to send you to *calmecac* for good." A wink seemed to be in order. "And I will miss you. But you will visit a lot. Like my brother did."

There were agitated voices, and a small army of slaves came running, bearing on them, their gesturing shaky, faces flustered. She felt Chimal tensing by her side, and she shivered too, recognizing the personal maid of the Empress in the lead.

"Honorable First Son, please follow," cried out the woman, her cheeks glowing red.

"What happened?" he whispered, resisting her pull.

"Oh, your father, the Emperor, he wants to see you. Come!"

Iztac just stood there, transfixed, the sensation of the looming disaster crawling up her spine. Something was wrong. Something was terribly amiss. The look that Chimal shot at her as he was pulled away confirmed the ominous feeling.

"What happened?" she asked the slave, who still lingered as if undecided, gazing around and at a loss.

The man looked up, as if finding it difficult to concentrate. "Oh, Honorable Second Wife, it's the Emperor," he cried out, wringing his hands. "He is dying!"

ABOUT THE AUTHOR

Zoe Saadia is the author of several novels on pre-Columbian Americas. From the architects of the Aztec Empire to the founders of the Iroquois Great League, from the towering pyramids of Tenochtitlan to the longhouses of the Great Lakes, her novels bring long-forgotten history, cultures and people to life, tracing pivotal events that brought about the greatness of North and Mesoamerica.

To learn more about Zoe Saadia and her work, please visit
www.zoesaadia.com

CPSIA information can be obtained
at www.ICGtesting.com
Printed in the USA
LVHW040001180323
741890LV00005B/37